How could a woman that gorgeous be so damned crazy?

Grabbing her arm, Levi dragged her away from the staring eyes. He turned on her. "Who are you?" They had just survived a scene right out of a high-octane action movie, 3-D stunts included. He was just a P.I. But she...she was no P.I. At least not one like he'd ever met.

This mission was of the utmost importance. But he wasn't moving from this spot until he knew the truth. "Who are you?"

He shouldn't have looked at her, not directly into her eyes like that. Maybe even then he could have maintained control. If she hadn't stared with such longing at his mouth. If the world had stopped turning at just that second. If something, anything, had happened. He might not have kissed her....

But he did and so did she....

DEBRA WEBB

CLASSIFIED

TORONTO NEW YORK LONDON
AMSTERDAM PARIS SYDNEY HAMBURG
STOCKHOLM ATHENS TOKYO MILAN MADRID
PRAGUE WARSAW BUDAPEST AUCKLAND

Secrets are sometimes meant to be kept. The pain caused is often not worth the change brought about by the revelation. We all keep secrets. Mostly the small things that are basically irrelevant (a new haircut or color is not so attractive on a colleague…that dress isn't flattering on a friend). Those little secrets are more about opinion than about hiding the facts. But some secrets are not so small and cannot be kept…they simply must reveal themselves. This book is dedicated to those who have faced a painful revelation and survived. Never lose your ability to trust and to believe!

ISBN-13: 978-0-373-74628-6

CLASSIFIED

Copyright © 2011 by Debra Webb

Recycling programs for this product may not exist in your area.

Printed in U.S.A.

ABOUT THE AUTHOR

Debra Webb wrote her first story at age nine and her first romance at thirteen. It wasn't until she spent three years working for the military behind the Iron Curtain and within the confining political walls of Berlin, Germany, that she realized her true calling. A five-year stint with NASA on the space shuttle program reinforced her love of the endless possibilities within her grasp as a storyteller. A collision course between suspense and romance was set. Debra has been writing romantic suspense and action-packed romantic thrillers since. Visit her at www.DebraWebb.com or write to her at P.O. Box 4889, Huntsville, AL 35815.

Books by Debra Webb

CAST OF CHARACTERS

Levi Stark—His mission is top secret. He must find the truth amid a web of deceit and danger spanning three decades.

Casey Manning—A CIA agent on probation, Casey is only too happy to accept the challenge her godfather, Lucas Camp, offers. The mission is classified.

Lucas Camp—He is desperate to find the real story on Slade Keaton. Lucas fears that Keaton represents a serious threat to his wife, Victoria, and to him.

Victoria Colby-Camp—She will do anything to protect her husband…even keep a secret. Will finding the truth about Slade Keaton destroy her marriage and perhaps her life?

Slade Keaton—He is the enigmatic head of the Equalizers, a private investigations firm that ensures justice outside the law as often as inside.

Paulo Fernandez—He is a simple man, or so it would seem. He knows many secrets and he appears willing to sell them to the highest bidder. But can he be trusted?

Alayna—No one knows her real name. She is beautiful and talented…but is she deadly?

Jazz—Alayna's personal assistant and only friend.

The Dragon—Pure evil. No one knows her name. She might be nothing more than a legend or myth in the intelligence world. But Lucas Camp and Slade Keaton know just how real and dangerous she is.

Jim Colby—He is the son of Victoria Colby-Camp, head of the Colby Agency. He has his reservations about Slade Keaton, however, no one understands secrets better than Jim. Whatever happens, he will protect his mother.

Ian Michaels and Simon Ruhl—Victoria's most trusted colleagues. These two men serve as seconds-in-command at the Colby Agency.

Chapter One

Chicago,
October 10, 10:15 p.m.

Lucas Camp waited in the shadows for his contact to show. Fog had rolled in along with the darkness, but that wasn't the catalyst propelling his tension to such a frustrating level. He shook his head. Nearly three decades of the cloak-and-dagger gig had jaded him, particularly when it came to the atmospheric musings of spy thrillers. Lucas had never feared what he could see and analyze. It was the unknown variable that set a man like him on edge, which was where he squarely stood now.

This business was more often brutal than romantic. He thought of his wife Victoria and he smiled. Yet there were moments when the unforgiving world of undercover operations proved worth every ounce of the relentless determination and nail-biting uncertainty one encountered. He and Victoria had survived much uncertainty and pain and no small amount of fear during more than two of those decades. Lucas would not trade a single second of his life now with his beloved Victoria to escape an eternity of the worst he had suffered to arrive at this place in their lives.

He shrugged off the creeping chill prompted more by what he'd come here to do than by the night's sharp warning that an early winter was imminent. Anger unfolded deep in his gut. For almost a year now he had sensed a simmering threat to his world. Endless digging had unearthed practically nothing on the source he suspected. And yet he understood that the truth was out there somewhere. The nagging instinct would not be assuaged.

Slade Keaton watched Lucas's every move. More disturbing, he had wormed his way into Victoria's good graces despite Lucas's persistent warnings. Even Jim, Victoria's son, had decided Keaton was perhaps not the potential risk both he and

Lucas had speculated. Since the Colby Agency's Fourth of July picnic just a few months ago, Keaton had become a frequent visitor at the agency as well as a guest at countless family functions.

Lucas intended to uncover the truth about Keaton no matter the measures required. He would not permit this enigma to permeate their lives any deeper without learning and understanding the precise threat. And there was a looming threat. No matter that the accused perpetrator behind the assassination attempt on his and Victoria's lives in Mexico just three weeks ago had been identified and brought to justice, Lucas knew deep in his gut that Keaton was somehow involved and that meant the case was still unsolved. The real perpetrator still out there. Lucas intended to prove his theory and stop the man. Victoria would be most unhappy if she were to discover Lucas's ongoing efforts to corroborate what she now perceived as a groundless theory.

In all their years together as a couple and as close friends before that, he had never set out to deceive or mislead his wife before; but he had little choice at this point. She insisted that they stop looking for trouble as far as Keaton was concerned. A man with an agenda would certainly have acted by now, she contended.

Victoria's attitude in terms of the passage of time without a substantiated incident linked to Keaton was not lost on Lucas. The mounting coincidences loosely involving Keaton, such as Victoria's abduction this past summer, no longer carried any weight in her opinion. Their years of investigating wrongdoing and protecting the innocent were to blame. She insisted they both needed to accept that undeniable fact. Lucas agreed...to a degree.

Still, something was off with Keaton, and Lucas intended to ferret out its root and the man's intent. Lucas would not rest until he had the facts.

As if his building impatience had telegraphed that urgency to his contact, a shadowy figure emerged from the fog. She wore the same dark attire as Lucas, from the leather jacket to the rubber-soled shoes designed for stealth. Some clichés simply worked in the real world as well as the make-believe one. Blending in to one's environment proved essential for many reasons, not the least of which was survival.

"My uncle warned me that you still practice that old-school methodology," the young woman said as she approached Lucas. The long, lush blond hair that had helped mark her as a true beauty since she was a teenager had been neatly tucked beneath an elegant fedora. "He wasn't wrong."

"Is he ever?" Lucas smiled as he opened his arms for a hug from his goddaughter.

Casey Manning hugged him hard and fast. "Lucas, it's good to see you." A broad smile spread across her lips. "As much as I love my uncle, you must know you've always been my idol."

He chuckled. "We won't tell Thomas about that."

Casey Manning was the niece of Thomas Casey, one of Lucas's oldest friends in the intelligence business. He, too, was a super spook, only he hadn't retired just yet. Since Thomas didn't have children of his own, his niece was like a daughter to him. As hard as he'd tried to dissuade her from joining the Central Intelligence Agency, she, like her uncle and her father, had been far too stubborn to listen. The government had gained another top-notch operative from the Casey lineage for that reason.

"So." Casey surveyed the deserted street then studied Lucas's face. "What's this covert rendezvous about? Uncle Thomas says you're worried that you've lost your objectivity on a mark."

Lucas had no intention of admitting any such thing, but Thomas Casey was nothing if not perceptive and honest in his analysis of a situation. "How about we go for a drive?" Lucas gestured to the sedan parked at the curb a few feet away. During business hours a curbside parking spot in downtown Chicago was about as easy to find as a taxi in a rainstorm. Fortunately at this hour the only traffic on the street one might encounter was the regularly scheduled patrol of Chicago P.D. or the occasional vagrant searching for lost and discarded treasures.

"As long as the route includes an all-night coffee shop you've got a deal." Casey crossed the sidewalk in three long strides.

"Already arranged." Lucas opened the

passenger door of his sedan. "Skinny, white chocolate mocha, if I recall correctly." The flavored coffee, tall size with fat-free milk, sat in the console's cup holder next to his own tall, Colombian roast, black coffee.

"A perfect example of what sets the men of your generation apart from mine." She dropped into the passenger seat and flashed Lucas another of those wide, completely uninhibited smiles. "You know how to treat a lady."

Lucas cast her a speculative look. "Is there a particular young man I need to teach a thing or two on your behalf?"

"Not necessary." She winked, mischief glittering in her blue eyes. "I've already taught him more than he wanted to know."

Lucas chuckled as he closed the car door. He doubted this young woman took any grief from men of any generation. Which was both a blessing and a curse. Her uncle worried that her jaded attitude toward relationships would leave her sad and alone. Like Thomas himself, he had admitted to Lucas over a few drinks not so long ago. Lucas knew that place all too well. Victoria had rescued him from a life of loneliness.

Once Lucas settled behind the steering wheel and started the engine, Casey cut to the chase.

"What's going on with this mark that you don't want Victoria to know about?" Casey cradled her cup of flavored coffee close to her face, allowing the warmth and rich aroma to infuse her senses.

His goddaughter knew him almost as well as her uncle. "He goes by the name Slade Keaton. He's been watching the Colby Agency—primarily Victoria and me—for almost a year. Maybe longer. I can't ignore my instincts on this guy."

"No overt threats?"

"Nothing I can pin down," Lucas admitted grudgingly. "There have been a number of incidents to which he has, one way or another, appeared connected, however vaguely." Lucas shook his head, frustrated that even as he made the statement he possessed not one specific event he could name as absolute. "The coincidences keep stacking up. Somehow he's involved."

"Victoria believes otherwise."

Lucas nodded. "He keeps drawing closer, always finding a way to be of assistance rather than the contrary. But it's wrong. I can feel it. I believe Victoria still has reservations but she wants peace. I don't want Keaton stealing another moment of that peace."

"You almost sound jealous, Lucas."

She studied him more closely, as if the meager glow of the street lamp would help her to confirm that perhaps on some level she was correct. The fact was, Keaton seemed to be in competition with Lucas for Victoria's attention. "Not jealous, just worried," he insisted. And that was the bottom line.

"What do you need me to do?"

"Three weeks ago Victoria and I were in Mexico for a second honeymoon. Despite the considerable security precautions we took we were attacked in the small village of Pozos."

"K and R?"

Kidnap-and-ransom attacks were a growing concern worldwide and Mexico remained a hotbed of that particular criminal activity. "Mexico's federal police suggested as much, but the incident didn't feel like a K and R attempt. It felt personal."

Casey snorted a laugh. "I'm sure the investigation conducted by the *federales* was very thorough. Their attempts are a joke most of the time. I'd put my money on your instincts."

He always did. "The Colby Agency followed up with its own investigation." For all the good it had done. Lucas continued to be amazed that his resources as well as the Colby Agency's consistently came up empty-handed where Keaton was concerned.

"You found nothing?"

Until this last time. "I discovered something," he allowed cautiously, "though it may be nothing." He wasn't prepared to discuss the woman he thought he'd seen in the crowd that morning in Puerto Vallarta. Lucas had found no indication that *she* was in the region. Nearly thirty years had passed since he'd seen her. They'd had no contact in that time. He had to have been mistaken. Besides, that part of his past was irrelevant. "A former member of the Colby Agency, Trevor Sloan, found a local who recognized Slade Keaton. Unfortunately, the man couldn't recall when he'd last seen Keaton."

"So you couldn't place him in the area during the ordeal."

Regrettably that was correct. "Just another of those loose threads." There had been far too many over the past year.

"Can Keaton account for his whereabouts during that time?"

"He claims he was on the West coast." Lucas had conducted his own investigation. The airline's paperwork confirmed that a man identified as Keaton had boarded each flight, and the hotel validated that person's five-day stay.

"Doesn't mean he wasn't involved," Casey offered, distracted. Like Lucas she would be mulling over the possibilities.

Exactly the argument Lucas had used with Victoria. "Finding that local who claimed to recognize Keaton is the first break I've had in my investigation into this man's history." Casey would understand just how profound that statement was.

"He's that good?"

"Or that bad," Lucas countered. "I want to know who he is." Lucas allowed a beat of silence to emphasize his request. "I want to know what he wants." Not once in his career had Lucas felt so…helpless. None of his resources had been able to provide the first inkling of intelligence on Keaton. His gut clenched at the memory of Jennifer Ashton taking her own life apparently because she couldn't help where Keaton was concerned. Or because what she had found had proven lethal to the messenger. That painful fact haunted Lucas every day.

"This is completely off the record with Victoria," he reminded Casey, guilt nipping at his insides. "I don't want her to worry." Or to be annoyed. Victoria didn't want Lucas stressing over this issue any longer.

"I got it," Casey assured him. "Mission classified. You have what I need to move forward?"

Lucas withdrew an envelope from his interior jacket pocket and passed it to her. "There's a photo of Keaton, along with his fingerprints and the shallow history he boasts as truth. And the name and location of the local in Pozos who claimed to know him. And, of course, the travel arrangements and adequate funds." Doubt swelled in his chest. "Your uncle explained that your safety is paramount. I don't want you taking any unnecessary risks. Find what you can without compromising your safety."

"You kidding?" she scoffed at his warning. "Didn't Uncle Thomas tell you? I'm bulletproof."

Lucas resisted the compulsion to caution her a second time but the effort would be wasted and unappreciated. Casey Manning had survived three near-death experiences in her young life. Lucas was thankful for her survival in each instance, but those same lucky breaks made her feel invincible. That was not a good thing in this business. In truth, Thomas was glad the Agency had taken her out of the field. With the worldwide political climate so volatile just now, having loved ones in the field was troubling. Casey, however, was most unhappy. This mission would be a stroll in the park for her. Maybe give her some perspective away from the danger of her typical CIA missions.

Lucas considered the threats and attempts he and Victoria had endured this last year and decided he might very well be wrong. This whole quest could be a terrible mistake for all involved.

He prayed he was wrong and that this mission wouldn't prove the most dangerous of his goddaughter's career.

Same time across town...

VICTORIA COLBY-CAMP WAITED for her investigator's reaction to her request. Time was running out. Lucas had said he would be home around midnight. She didn't want to have to explain why she had stayed at the office so late. Lucas was far too perceptive. Time was of the essence in solving this case as well. Recent events had confirmed her worst fears.

Slade Keaton was up to something and he certainly was not who he claimed.

"When do I leave?" Levi Stark asked.

Relief filtered through Victoria. Stark was the perfect investigator for the job and she was glad he had agreed to take the assignment despite its being off the record. He was well trained and more than qualified. That he had an eye for art made him even more invaluable under the circumstances. The small Mexican village of Pozos had lured many artists. He would fit in well. From Victoria's perspective he was the perfect choice since he was the newest member of her staff, though nearly two years had passed since he'd first sat before her desk for an interview. A great deal of that time had been spent in the research department, not in the field.

"I've made arrangements for tomorrow midmorning. Will that work for you?" It had taken Victoria more than two weeks to work out the details as well as to summon the resolve to do this behind Lucas's back. She cringed inwardly. The sooner it was over the better she would feel. She had deceived Lucas only once and, like this time, it had been for his own good. The last time she had been faced with the possibility that she had a terrible disease and she hadn't wanted to worry her family until the doctor's suspicions were confirmed. Fortunately the test results triggering the concern had been falsified for another's own agenda. Keeping Lucas in the dark that time had resulted in her being abducted and held in a mental institution. Victoria hoped there would be a vastly different result this time.

Though this was an entirely different situation, there were similarities. Lucas could be in danger. After what they'd gone through in Mexico, Victoria needed to be sure about Slade Keaton. Lucas remained firm in his assessment that Keaton was not who or what he said. Victoria had not been as convinced until the incident in Pozos. The attempt on her and her husband's lives below the border had been one too many twists of fate with Keaton's name, however obscurely, in the mix. Victoria had watched over these last months the toll that uncertainty took on Lucas. She wanted the issues surrounding Keaton's identity and motives resolved once and for all. Going to Jim or having Sloan follow up would have been the easiest, but neither of the two would have been willing to keep Lucas out of the loop.

This is the best way. This time.

"Tomorrow is fine, ma'am," Stark said. "What's my cover?"

"Mineral de Pozos was a mecca during

the silver mining boom. But like many other places, when the mining heyday ended hard times fell upon the area, leaving it little more than a ghost town. Recently revitalization has begun, due to the low real estate prices that have attracted many artists."

"I see." He nodded. "My mother is an artist."

"That background provides an opportunity for you to question the locals without stirring suspicions." The Colby Agency had a reputation for hiring not only the very best investigators and security specialists but also those with diverse backgrounds. The combination was unparalleled in the business of private investigations. Victoria and her son Jim strived to maintain that superior balance at the agency.

"I agree. I appreciate the opportunity."

Levi Stark had moved to Chicago from his home state of Florida nearly two years ago. He still hadn't adjusted to the climate change but he'd meshed perfectly with the staff here at the agency. His work in the Colby Agency's research department had been so outstanding that Victoria had been tempted to try and persuade him to stay there. But, like most who came to the agency, he had wanted to become a field investigator in time.

"Excellent. Your contact for resources once you arrive is in the case file. He will provide whatever you need. I'd like you to keep me posted as often as possible." Victoria suffered a twinge of doubt. This case, as she'd briefed Stark, sounded inordinately straightforward and quite simple. Yet, she feared it would not be nearly so. Lucas wasn't alone when it came to suffering those troubling doubts related to Keaton. "Take extraordinary care, Stark. Your safety is to be your first priority."

"Understood."

"And Lucas cannot know." The words left a bitter taste in her mouth, but they were necessary. This was something to which Victoria needed to attend, discreetly and promptly. Whatever Keaton's obsession with Lucas, she intended to ensure he meant no harm.

"You're the boss. Off the record it is."

With that Levi Stark left Victoria's office, the case file under his arm.

He would follow the leads he found until the truth about Slade Keaton was revealed. As far as the rest of the agency would know, Stark was on vacation. Lucas would be most displeased that she had taken this route if he learned of her actions. As much as she regretted the need to mislead him in this way, Victoria had been in this business far too long not to trust her intuition. She wasn't wasting another minute.

For better or worse…it was done.

Chapter Two

Mineral de Pozos, Mexico,
October 11, 2:30 p.m.

Casey Manning wandered onto the verandah outside her room at the Hacienda de Pozos. The sun felt good on her face. Locally designed and crafted wind chimes tinkled in the faint breeze. The view was nothing short of inspiring. Pozos presented a fascinating clash of ancient history and modern revival. Revitalized structures filled with contemporary art were shoehorned between stark ruins from the days when this ghost town had been a booming source of silver. Lucky for Casey, the hotel sat on a slight rise above the town plaza, providing an excellent surveillance opportunity of the activities beyond. Bougainvillea was draped like a necklace along the railing where she stood overlooking an al fresco dining space that reminded her of her childhood home in Southern California.

Soon the music in the cantina below would fill the cooler evening air and she would wander among the patrons in search of her first mark. The Well was his favorite watering hole and he socialized there most nights.

Paulo Fernandez was forty-nine, though he looked sixty. Goats and chickens were his livelihood in Pozos. To his neighbors and customers he was the old man who'd turned the church ruins on the edge of town into goat and chicken pens. The same old man whose dried meat shop in the main plaza kept his patrons coming back. Fernandez's outwardly one-dimensional character ran far deeper than anyone recognized. Based on Casey's research she would wager his ancestors had been traitors in the Mexican Revolution at the beginning of the twentieth century and not much had changed through the generations since. Fernandez played snitch for the *federales* or whoever else paid the largest sum of pesos. He hadn't inherited the old mining hacienda he called home as most believed. His lucrative little side job had paid for the property and the renovations.

Casey knew and understood his type. Ruthlessness camouflaged by charm. Relentlessness hidden by humility. She could handle Fernandez with both eyes shut. With a quick check of her cell, which had succumbed to poor service but still maintained the time, she headed down to the lobby to meet her resource. She had arrived as prepared as legally possible but some necessities wouldn't pass airport screening. For those essentials she required a local resource. Central Mexico hadn't been among her assignments thus far in her CIA career but a quick call to a colleague had provided a name and number for the best man in the region.

Casey strolled across the cobblestone courtyard, admiring the beautifully aged architecture adorned by the late season's blooms until she spotted the red silk scarf that tagged her contact. In this case the best man in the region was a woman. Tall, elegant and with a lush mane of coal-black hair cascading down her back, Eva Sanchez sat at a table sipping a tall glass of what appeared to be water with a lemon wedge perched on the rim. A large colorful and clearly expensive bag sat at her feet. The stilettos and flowing white skirt with matching ballerina blouse gave her the look of a chic contessa. The red scarf offered an eye-catching pop of color that few could ignore. Their gazes locked and Casey crossed to her table.

"Ms. Manning, you're far younger than I expected." Eva smiled, gesturing to the chair opposite her and then to her glass. "Would you like a drink? I recommend the sparkling water. It's immensely refreshing and it is by far the safest of the things you will encounter while visiting our lovely country."

"I'm good, thanks." Casey settled into the chair. "You had no problems filling my order?" There were times when small talk served a purpose but this was not one of those times. Casey wasn't here to make friends. She was extraordinarily gifted at setting aside her emotions. Her last boyfriend had reveled in pointing out what he called a deep-seated personality flaw.

"I have everything you need." Sanchez's expression shifted to one of business. "Two handguns. One Beretta 9mm and one Ruger .22 caliber. A holster for the latter. One box of rounds for each. One four-inch switchblade."

"You received my cash transfer?" Payment up front—that was the deal. No exceptions.

"Of course." Sanchez flashed another of those practiced smiles that fell short of her eyes. "Otherwise I would not be here." She drew a small red clutch purse from the larger bag at her feet and placed cash on the table for her tab. "All is as it should be."

"Excellent."

Sanchez openly studied Casey for a moment. "Be very careful, Ms. Manning. Human trafficking has reached an all-time high in our country. You fit the most highly sought-after profile. Watch your back." She rose with all the grace of a well-trained dancer. "And good luck with your venture."

Casey pushed out of her own chair, while not as gracefully as the other woman with every bit as much barefaced confidence. "Thanks." She didn't bother mentioning that she never relied on luck to accomplish her mission. Luck was for those incapable of getting the job done on their own.

When Sanchez had disappeared beyond the arched entry gates, Casey picked up the fashionable bag she'd left behind and headed back to her room. There was no need to check the merchandise for quality; Sanchez was a five-star resource. Not an easy accomplishment. The designation signified that Sanchez not only came through with high quality merchandise every time, she did so even when her personal safety was at risk.

A woman after Casey's own heart. Any mission that didn't include some level of danger would surely be incredibly boring and intensely unproductive.

The Well, 9:45 p.m.

THE MUSIC WAS LOUD, the lights low. The blazing logs in the broad stone fireplace kept the evening chill at bay. Every chair and stool in the house was occupied. Bearing in mind that the Well might be the only decent cantina for fifty miles, the crowd was no surprise and actually suited Casey's objective for the evening. Fernandez was here. She had watched him work the crowd like an oily politician running for office. He'd permitted a brief glance in her direction, making a mental note of her position, as any experienced informant would. She was armed. He would expect as much. The .22 nestled snugly against her right thigh in its leather holster. What he wouldn't expect was the switchblade strapped to her other thigh with a silk scarf. Eva Sanchez wasn't the only one who knew how to put silk to good use. The wide-bottomed bohemian skirt covered both well and allowed for quick, easy access.

Casey ordered another sparkling water and waited for Fernandez to get around to her. He was in no hurry; he knew she would wait. Let him enjoy his moment of power. She needed information. Playing nice was her role tonight. The CIA had taught her well the art of assuming roles and maintaining patience. This was the easy part.

Eventually Fernandez swaggered up to the bar next to her. "Ah, Miss Manning." Though he spoke English, the accent was thick with salsa flavor and his emphasis leaned heavily on the *miss*.

Casey turned to face the man who claimed to have some knowledge of Slade Keaton. "Mr. Fernandez." She offered her hand for a nice-to-meet-you shake and he proceeded to cradle it for a mini-eternity before planting a light kiss there. If she hadn't read his background she would have been surprised by his skill at impersonating a suave gentleman. But she wasn't. At all.

A brief visual exchange between Fernandez and the man seated next to Casey had him vacating the bar stool. Fernandez slid into his place. "Shall we get down to business, *chiquita,* or do you prefer foreplay?"

A sense of humor, too. How nice. "Is that code for 'you have additional information for me'?" Perhaps to some Fernandez might be viewed as quite the ladies' man in his white linen trousers and scarcely buttoned cotton shirt, both emphasizing his dark features, but not to a SoCal girl who'd just dumped her lying, cheating boyfriend.

Her contact's laugh harmonized with the frisky Latin music. Then, with a single blink of his eyes, he changed modes and all signs of amusement vanished from his face. He leaned in close to her. "You will be pleased to know that the person you seek is more than a friend to Señor Keaton. She claims to be his *hermana*."

Sister? That was interesting. If genuine, the familial connection could carry added benefit. "Do you have any verification of what she asserts?" Casey shrugged and stirred her water with the thin pink straw that bobbed next to the lemon wedge. "I'm not in the market for hearsay unless there's an element of corroboration."

Fernandez lifted two fingers to the bartender before meeting her eyes once more. "I can neither confirm nor refute anything she claims. I can, however," he added when Casey would have interrupted, "attest that this woman has lived at the same address, used the same name and operated the same business for several years. Her former lover was a nephew of a lady I once knew *very* well." He leaned even closer as he said the last. "This claim is nothing new and I have never heard rumors to the contrary. Although, I have heard that the name Slade

Keaton is an alias. Regrettably, I have no knowledge of his given name."

A warning fired in Casey's veins. This was another of those coincidences Lucas had spoken of. A man who had this level of knowledge about someone who knew Keaton just happened to live in the town where Victoria and Lucas had visited and been attacked. Not so likely. More significant, the man—Fernandez—just happened to be the sort who would sell his own mother's soul to the devil if the price was right. Too convenient.

The bartender plopped two shot glasses glistening with golden tequila on the counter in front of Fernandez. He nodded his approval before sliding one toward Casey. "A toast to our mutually beneficial business." He gestured to the waiting glass. "This is the best tequila in all the land."

Casey reached past the glass he'd slid her way and snagged the one he'd kept for himself. She held it up. *"Salute."*

Another of those charming laughs echoed from him as he lifted the glass she'd refused and echoed her toast before downing the contents in a single swallow.

Casey knocked back the shot of tequila then honed in on his dark watchful gaze. "I need a name and an address. As previously agreed, half the money up front, the other half when I confirm your uncorroborated claims about her identity."

"Yes, those are the previously agreed terms." Fernandez placed the glass on the counter. "For certain I would be most happy to complete our business tonight. But…" He sighed. Casey didn't hear the sound but she saw the exaggerated inhale-and-exhale. "Unfortunately I cannot do business with you when you are cursed with a tracker." He threw up his hands. "Particularly one wanting the same information as you. I find myself in a very—as you Americans say—sticky situation."

Casey sat up straighter, her instincts going on alert. "What're you talking about, Fernandez?" She had known this was too easy. Her pulse rate elevated.

"The *gringo* at the back table dressed in the blue jacket and snakeskin boots."

She glanced in that direction. In three seconds flat she noted several things about the man. Not much older than her, late twenties, thirty. Dark hair. He looked American, then again that was not unusual in Pozos. Most of the artists who'd taken up residence were American. But this one had been asking about Keaton.

And he was watching Casey.

"Shake your American friend," Fernandez tossed at her, "and we can do business."

Her contact ambled away, merging with the other patrons and falling into conversation as if he'd never left the festivities.

Who the heck was this party crasher? She glared openly at the stranger in the blue jacket and hoped he felt the animosity all the way across the smoky room.

Only one way to find out. Casey snagged a bill from her shoulder bag and deposited it on the bar. She weaved her way through the tables and standing patrons until she reached the guy's table. He watched her coming, making no move to escape a confrontation or to even stand to greet her, for that matter. Where were all the men like Lucas and her uncle Thomas?

Casey flattened her palms on the stranger's table and leaned down close enough to identify the nice aftershave he wore. The man had taste and the funds to back it up, it seemed. "We need to talk." His eyes were green. Really, really green. Emerald green. She blinked and gave herself a prompt mental kick. His eyes were green. So what?

He studied her a moment with those emerald eyes. "Do I know you?"

Despite the spirited music blaring in the background, the uncommonly deep sound of his voice made Casey shiver as if the night air had somehow cut through the warmth of the room and splashed chill bumps across her skin. She shook it off. *Focus.* What kind of game was he playing?

"If you don't," she warned, "you're about to become intimately acquainted."

He smiled. Just a smile. Wide, open and fiercely attractive. Casey ordered herself to breathe.

"Why don't you join me?" He indicated the vacant chair at his table.

Fury whiplashed Casey, booting her from amateur land. What the heck was wrong with her? Maybe the place and the music or the ridiculous concept that she was still furious at her ex and revenge was baiting her with the idea that this guy was nothing short of *hot*.

"Outside." She didn't wait to see if he intended to follow the order. Seriously ticked off at herself and *his* intrusion into *her* mission, she executed an about-face, worked her way through the crowd and out the door.

Too many eyes and ears in the courtyard, she observed. Beyond the arched entry that welcomed guests and patrons to the hotel grounds, the street was empty. Good. He was behind her. Not that he made a sound; his movements were remarkably soundless. She could feel him.

The street corner would work. As she approached that mark, Casey reached under her skirt and snatched the .22 from its holster, then wheeled to face the annoying glitch in her plan. Rather than meeting his green eyes beneath the moonlight, her gaze locked on the business end of a sleek 9mm.

Well, well. She would have thought of this if she hadn't been so busy analyzing his eyes and smile. What a stupid mistake!

"Who're you?" he demanded.

"Ladies first," Casey fired back. "Who

are you and why are you following me?"
She tightened her grip on the .22 and widened her stance. Shooting him on the street like this wasn't exactly how she'd planned her evening but she could be flexible when the need arose.

His gaze narrowed. "Who said I was following you? I just arrived in Pozos today. If you mean now, you invited me."

Yeah, right. "Do you always vacation armed?"

"What makes you think I'm on vacation?"

He had her there. "Lower your weapon and I'll lower mine."

The hesitation was understandable but his next move surprised her.

He lowered his weapon.

She almost laughed out loud. Now he was being stupid. Bad move.

Casey kicked the weapon from his hand and moved in. "Who are you?" she demanded, the muzzle of her .22 rammed into the underside of his chin.

"Let me introduce you." The male voice came from behind her.

Casey's brain analyzed and identified

the voice a split second after recognizing the sensation of a steel barrel boring into the back of her skull.

"Get his weapon," Fernandez ordered as he claimed Casey's .22. "Ensure that he carries no others."

"Hands up, *pendejo,*" the sidekick with Fernandez ordered as he poked the emerald-eyed stranger in the back with enough force to have him stumbling forward, face-first into her.

Absorbing the impact of his body with a grunt, Casey backed into Fernandez who nudged her with the weapon as a reminder that he had the upper hand. "We had a deal," she said over her shoulder. Was there no honor at all among his kind?

"I," he said as he grabbed a handful of her hair and jerked her head back, "have a deal that supersedes yours, *chiquita.*"

That certainly explained everything. "I'll pay you double whatever *he* is paying you." Whoever Green Eyes was, he wasn't about to one-up Casey Manning. She didn't care if he had made his deal first.

"Triple," Green Eyes countered, his gaze

glued to Casey's, his hands in the air while Fernandez's cohort frisked him.

Who the hell was this guy? Ignoring the muzzle biting into her scalp, Casey twisted to face Fernandez. His ruthless grip tightened in her hair. She gritted her teeth to restrain a wince. "You double-cross me and you won't live to regret it, my friend." Anger, mostly at herself, scorched away any trace of common sense she had left. Kicking this guy's butt was going to feel so good. *Even if it kills you?* Her uncle's voice echoed in her ears.

Fernandez snorted. "Perhaps you are the one who will not live to regret it."

"Watch out!" Green Eyes shouted a split second before a blow rattled Casey's brain.

Pain shattered her skull. Her mind willed her to strike back but the blackness swallowed her too fast.

She was down.

Chapter Three

She wasn't dead.

That was good.

Maybe. Levi wasn't so sure. So far this woman appeared as much an enemy as the guys driving the truck but since she and Levi were in the same predicament he'd give her the benefit of the doubt.

The pickup bumped over the rutted road, tossing him against the woman. He tried to roll away from her but with his hands and feet bound, he had little control over his movements.

He had no idea who she was. Fernandez had refused to give her name when he and Levi had conducted their first on-site meeting. Levi had tried getting a shot of her with his cell phone to send to Victoria at the agency for possible identification but this chick was too smart for that. She stayed meshed with her surroundings, limiting photo ops. He couldn't exactly send the description that best suited her. Long, silky blond hair and radiant blue eyes, and a body that made her hard to ignore. Lean but with just the slightest gentle curves in all the right places. The woman was striking, there was no denying. Levi savored a deep breath of her scent. And she smelled like flowers right after a rain. Not a gaudy, cloying scent. A delicate, honeyed fragrance that had him leaning closer when he knew better.

As good as she smelled that didn't mean she wasn't as thorny as the award-winning roses his mother nurtured in her garden back in Tallahassee.

Another bounce of the truck and Levi rolled against her, a little harder this time. She groaned and her eyes fluttered open. It took a second or two for her to assess the situation before he felt the tension ripple through her. She started to squirm. Not exactly an unpleasant thing but definitely a dangerous one.

"Hey, hey!" he whispered, infusing as

much urgency as possible into his tone. "Take it easy." If she started screaming the driver would likely stop to shut her up. For good this time. With his hands tied behind his back Levi couldn't stop her from yelling if she decided to go for it. "Don't scream, okay?" He held his breath, braced for the worst.

She stilled. No screaming, thankfully. He dared to breathe.

"I don't know where they're taking us," he explained, "but I'm reasonably certain they intend this moonlight drive to be our last ride."

There wasn't enough light to read her expression much less her eyes as she analyzed his warning for a beat or two. "Who are you?"

Persistent, wasn't she? They really didn't have time for this but if it would gain her cooperation for now it would be worth the inconvenience. "I'm a private detective. I believe we're looking for the same person." She started to squirm again. "I'm not your enemy," he reassured her. She ignored him and kept wiggling. She was going to get them killed earlier than already scheduled.

"If you draw their attention—"

Before he finished the warning she had fidgeted around until her bound hands were behind her bent knees. With some soft swearing and more struggling she worked until she slipped her right leg free of the loop her arms made, then she did the same with her left.

No way could he achieve that move.

Before he had stopped marveling at her spectacular physical feat, she rummaged around beneath her skirt. There was a metal clunk, more scrambling with her hands, and finally a distinct click he recognized. That could be trouble. For him.

"Turn over."

His full attention fixed on the knife in her hand.

"Turn over," she repeated.

Levi rolled onto his right side. If he was lucky she was about to cut him loose. If he wasn't, she might be about to bury the blade to the hilt. The decision required little weighing. He would take his chances with her any day over the *hombres* in the cab. At the very least she would be easier to subdue. Maybe. The sawing action against the ropes constricting his wrists permitted a fraction of relief.

"Now do me."

That was an invitation he would gladly accept now and later. Levi had to remind himself that, from what he knew, the lady was as likely to shoot him as she was to do anything else. She'd drawn her weapon first back there. She might not be as easy to subdue as she looked. She had acted quite fearless.

Exiling those concerns for now, he rolled back to his left and accepted the small switchblade. Waiting through a couple of bucks of the pickup was necessary before sliding the blade between her tightly bound wrists. The instant she was free she rubbed at the chafed skin. Levi quickly cut through the bindings around his ankles then reached for hers. She trembled when he touched her.

Soft. Her skin was soft and smooth as if she'd carefully shaved her legs then massaged them with lotion in anticipation of him touching her.

Did he really just think that?

The desert's night air had obviously

drugged him. Or maybe it was that subtle sweet scent of hers.

Another crazy notion. *Okay, Stark, get it together.* He sliced through the ropes, then closed the switchblade.

"I'll hang on to that." She took the knife from him and prepared to sit up.

"I wouldn't do that." Before his mush for brains could form a coherent thought and stop him, he'd grabbed her and pulled her back down beside him.

She jerked free of his hold. "You grab me like that again and I'll—"

"They have guns," he warned in case she didn't recall. "If we move around or try to jump out and they notice—which they will—they'll shoot."

"You're suggesting we just lie here and wait for them to take us wherever they want?"

Sounded lame when she put it that way. "I'm suggesting we maintain the element of surprise. They won't expect us to have gotten loose or to have a weapon. When they stop and come back for us, we'll make the first strike." Speaking of which… "Are you going to be able to use that knife when the time comes?" Fair question.

She laughed. If it hadn't annoyed the devil out of him he might have liked the throaty, honest sound of it.

"Look, mister, I don't know who you are—"

"Levi Stark." He hadn't gotten to his name before. She had a way of cutting him off like that. "My name is Levi Stark and I'm well trained in the use of weapons." The Colby Agency ensured top-notch training before turning investigators loose in the field.

"Glad to hear it, Stark." She slumped onto her back. "But I'll take my chances with my own training."

It was her switchblade; the choice was hers. "You didn't tell me your name." If they were about to fight or die together, perhaps both, knowing her name would make the circumstances a bit more civil.

"Casey," she said with a long look in his direction. "Casey Manning."

Nice name. "We can check the bed of the truck, moving around as little as possible, and see if we can find anything usable as a weapon."

"Stellar idea."

At least they agreed on one thing.

Keeping their movements as controlled and minimal as possible, each searched one side of the truck bed from cab to tailgate. The truck was old and there was plenty of filth, but not much else. Finally Levi's fingers encountered cold steel. They curled around the object and he grinned. Just what he'd hoped for. He scooted back to Casey, swaying with the jarring ride.

When he was close enough, she said, "I found a whole lot of nothing. You?"

"Tire iron." He was looking forward to using it after the way those two locos had whacked Casey. A frown tugged at his lips. He hadn't even asked about that. "How's your head?" Chances were she had a colossal headache and a nice lump to show for her lack of cooperation.

"Hurts." She rubbed at the back of her head. "No real damage."

"Good." He had to wonder at her training. Arguing with an armed man, especially when the muzzle was right in your face, was not a smart move.

"There's a sizeable hole in your strategy, Stark."

"What hole?" His plan was markedly better than jumping from a moving vehicle in the dark or informing the bad guys that they'd gotten loose. If she had a better one, she should speak up.

"When they realize we're not secured, the element of surprise will no longer be ours. I estimate that'll take about three seconds."

She had him there. "Good point." He considered a way around that strategic error. "I guess we'll just have to tie each other up again."

"I'll take care of our feet."

Before he could offer to do it, she scooted down to handle the task. If she had noticed his fascination with her ankles he doubted she wanted him in that position again. It was bad enough he recognized his own idiocy, he'd prefer not to show it off.

"We can hold the ropes around our wrists." She settled in next to him once more. "Did you overhear anything about where they're taking us?"

Levi stared out at the passing landscape. The stars and moon were helpful but nothing about the dark, desolate terrain gave him a clue as to where they were headed. And his command of the Spanish language wasn't that noteworthy. "The best I could understand, the destination is an abandoned mine."

"That could be anywhere around here," she muttered, clearly annoyed. "They're all over the place."

The truck slowed, then turned to the left. Tension screwed tighter inside him. "I guess we'll know soon enough." He tucked the tire iron into his waistband at his side and hoped the jacket would cover it sufficiently and that it wouldn't fall out.

"One question."

He turned to her, tried to read her face in the moonlight. "What's that?"

"If we overtake these guys, what's to keep you from overtaking me? Or trying anyway?" she added with a note of challenge that didn't quite rise to the occasion.

Was that vulnerability he heard in her

voice? "You have the knife," he reminded her. His protective instincts stirred though he felt reasonably certain she could take care of herself.

"You have the tire iron," she countered.

"Wanna trade?" he offered. It wasn't the time to be joking around and she was a stranger. Competition, it seemed. But he was pretty sure they both needed a break in the tension.

"I'll stick with the knife." She released a breathy sound, almost a laugh. "No pun intended."

The truck rocked to a stop.

"Showtime," she murmured.

The engine remained idling but the men's raised voices were audible above the rumble. Levi tried to make out some part of the conversation. Now he wished he had taken the time to master Spanish years ago. It didn't take a linguist, however, to recognize the two were in strict disagreement.

"The driver wants the other guy to do this while he waits in the truck."

He shouldn't have been, but Levi was impressed. Another expedient skill of hers. The passenger side door creaking open prevented him from offering a compliment and sticking his foot deeper into his mouth. This woman, Casey Manning, was his rival first and foremost. Caution was advisable.

The tailgate flopped open.

Casey stiffened next to him.

The guy, in a gray sweatshirt and jeans, said something in Spanish. Didn't sound positive. That it was the guy in the sweatshirt rather than the other one was preferable. The driver, the one in the striped shirt, seemed to be in charge and had apparently garnered that position with an extra measure of ruthlessness.

The man in the sweatshirt grabbed Casey by the ankles and dragged her forward. She screamed as if she were frightened. Levi was relatively certain she wasn't quite that scared. She wanted her captor off guard. The man cut the rope around her ankles and yanked her to her feet. She staggered away from him. He waved the pistol in his other hand and told her not to move. That part Levi understood perfectly. Casey froze as ordered.

Levi was next. When his feet hit the ground, he backed up to stand near Casey.

Another string of Spanish accompanied by a magnanimous gesture had Casey moving away from the truck and road. Levi followed. A flashlight clicked on, its beam cutting through the darkness. Cactus scrub and eroded sandy landscape stretched out before them, interrupted occasionally by crumbling stone and brick ruins. A low-slung moon showcased the Sierra Gorda Mountains and the foothills that stretched toward them. They kept walking. The pickup was a couple hundred yards behind them now but still visible.

Casey suddenly stumbled and fell to her knees on the ground. Levi squeezed his hands into fists to prevent releasing the ropes and reaching for her. The timing had to be right.

The bastard in the sweatshirt kicked at her. Levi locked his jaw. She wailed as if she were seriously injured and couldn't get up. Shouting a mixture of Spanish and English profanities, the jerk shoved the flashlight under his arm and grabbed her. He had put his knife into his pocket as soon as he'd freed their feet in the truck, but he still held a gun.

Levi made his move. He grabbed the guy in a choke hold and snatched at the gun with his free hand. Got it. The man twisted and squirmed and tried to grab at Levi. The flashlight dropped to the ground, its beam bouncing to a stop. Thirty seconds more and the pressure on the man's throat rendered him unconscious. Levi let go and he crumpled to the ground.

"Why didn't you just hit him?" Casey grumbled as she grabbed the flashlight.

"If the blow hadn't put him down," Levi argued, "he might have gotten off a shot." Taking him down and assuming control of the weapon simultaneously was the right choice for the situation. "What were you doing while I was taking him down?" She could have jumped in any time.

She ignored the question and glanced toward the truck. "The driver's getting out. We have to run."

Gunfire erupted. Two, then three shots hit the sand a few feet away.

Levi rushed after Casey who'd already covered some major ground. She'd turned off the flashlight which basically left them running blind but it was way better than providing easy targets.

"We should head in different directions," she suggested as he moved up next to her in a dead run.

Not a bad idea since the driver was still attempting to hit a target, but Levi wasn't taking the risk that she would give him the slip. Since she hadn't jumped in back there he had to assume she had no plans to play partner with him.

More gunfire shattered the silence. He considered stopping and returning fire but that would mean losing pace with Casey. She was after the same thing he was and Levi needed to know why. His boss would want to know as well.

Determined not to lose Casey to an abrupt diversionary tactic, he grabbed her by the arm and held on when she tried to shake him off.

"What're you doing?"

"Making sure you don't get away."

She didn't waste energy arguing, just kept running.

Keeping pace alongside her, he almost stumbled when the sandy dirt beneath their feet changed to something bouncy. The sound of wood splitting pierced the air

"Wait." Casey stopped. She turned to him, gave him a shove with her free hand but he wasn't letting go of her. Before he could regain his balance she went down. Levi lunged forward, dragged by her downward momentum.

His legs dangling into a deep hole in the earth, he held tight on to Casey's arm with one hand, while he grabbed the nearest cactus scrub with the other. As Casey's arm started to slip through his grasp, the air stalled in his lungs. His fingers clamped down on her wrist.

Got her.

What the heck had just happened? Casey hung like a rag doll from his grip on her wrist. Splintered wood jabbed at his chest. His entire being shook with the effort of clutching this clump of flora. They'd fallen into a…mine shaft, that's what happened. The weapon he'd confiscated had either gone down the hole or was on the ground somewhere.

A roar blasted through the night. The truck. Levi listened for any other sound.

No more gunfire. Apparently, the driver had decided to cut his losses.

"Can you pull me up?" Casey shouted.

He pulled hard on the scrub. Boards creaked. The old shaft had been covered in wooden boards that were now dry rotted, allowing them to collapse beneath his and Casey's weight. There was nothing reliable to grab besides the scrub. Not that he could have turned loose of the plant anyway. His mind scrambled for a solution.

"Can't do it." The admission didn't come easy but this was no time for vanity. His right shoulder was feeling the burden of hanging on to her in this awkward position. He tuned out the ache. Didn't matter if his shoulder ripped out of its socket. He couldn't let go.

Silence thickened for two, then three beats.

"If you can't pull us both up, then let me go."

"Are you nuts?" He wasn't letting go as long as he was able to hold on. No way.

"If we both fall there won't be anyone to go for help." She hesitated a moment. "We don't know how deep this thing is. I dropped the flashlight so I can't check it out. At any rate, there's a big possibility that we'll be injured in the fall. The best way out of this is for you to let go of me and head back to town for help."

She was crazy. He tightened his grip on her wrist. "Not happening, lady." He gritted his teeth against the strain ripping through his shoulder.

"This isn't the time to be a hero, Stark. Let me go and get help. We're both screwed if you don't."

Levi closed his eyes and tried with all his might to pull his torso up onto the ground. An inch forward, two back. Damn it! He growled in frustration.

She twisted her arm in an attempt to loosen his grip. "I said let go."

"No way," he roared. "Just be still and give me time to figure this out." Despite the cool night air sweat oozed from every pore of his body.

"Wait."

Levi ordered his respiration to slow so he could hear. His heart pounded so loud in his ears he could hardly hear his own thoughts.

"There's a ledge. I think I can make it."

Hope welled in his chest. Thank God.

She moved around. He grimaced at the pain now searing through his shoulder.

"Got it. You can let go now."

She sounded calm, as if she might even be telling the truth. But she wasn't. "If that's true, why aren't you holding your own weight?" The tug of her weight on his arm hadn't eased in the slightest. She was lying.

She swore, long and loud. He almost laughed. She wanted to be the hero instead of him. Talk about competitive. Granted she did have a point about going for help… but he wasn't letting her go.

A weight stamped on his hand—the one desperately grasping the scrub.

Levi's attention flew upward. The guy he'd put down in a choke hold stood over him, growling in Spanish. Oh hell.

"What's going on?" Casey demanded.

Levi couldn't answer. And he couldn't fight the guy without letting go of something. The only thing he could do was ignore the pain of each booted stamp on his hand and arm.

And hang on.

The SOB grabbed Levi's wrist with both hands and pulled to loosen his grip on the clump of scrub. "Die, *gringos!*" he screamed.

Don't let go. Levi focused on clamping harder even as his fingers were ripped from their desperate hold. Levi clutched at the bastard's leg.

The bastard twisted free.

Levi grappled at the sand…at the splintered wood…

Until his fingers closed on air.

Chapter Four

Victoria Colby-Camp put her toothbrush away and studied her reflection. She'd taken her hair down from the French twist she wore every day. It hung well past her shoulders. The silver streaks had multiplied quickly these past few years. Her dark eyes remained clear. She had stayed fit and, frankly, she didn't look so old. But sometimes she had to admit how very tired she felt.

The attack in Pozos on top of the abduction just a few months ago weighed heavily on her. Was it past time she and Lucas retired completely? She worried as much for her husband as for herself. Certainly her son Jim could run the Colby Agency without her at his side. Lucas was there more to be near Victoria than anything else.

Why not let Jim take the helm? She and Lucas could spend more time with their grandchildren. They could certainly do more traveling. Perhaps if she and Lucas put more distance between them and the business of investigations they could finally escape the sometimes dangerous and always unpredictable world in which they had both undeniably thrived for decades.

The idea scared Victoria just a little. Nearly thirty years of running the Colby Agency had for the most part been her life, particularly during those years while her son was missing and following her first husband's death. Did she really know anything else? She took a breath and steadied herself. Far more terrifying tasks had been conquered in the past. Besides, retirement was no enemy to her or her husband.

Emotion crowded her chest. Still, could she really leave Chicago? That was the only way to really distance herself from the business. Goose bumps spread over her skin like prickly reminders of all the emotion that would accompany such a decision.

Victoria pushed away the troubling thoughts and padded from the en suite to join her husband in bed. He tossed the newspaper aside and tucked his reading glasses on the bedside table.

Lucas saved the newspaper and the books he enjoyed for bedtime. That was the only time one would catch the man wearing a pair of reading glasses. Victoria had to smile, her insides softening with affection. Her husband was one of a kind. She wasn't so sure they made men like him anymore.

Drawing back the covers, Lucas welcomed her into their bed. He pulled her close and she snuggled into her special place next to him. Their bodies fit together perfectly. This was where she belonged.

Wherever they lived, whatever they did, that would never change.

Chapter Five

Mexico

Casey groaned. She reached up to touch her aching head. What the heck happened?

"Don't move."

Stark. At least they were both alive. It was dark. Pitch-black dark. The memory came back. They'd fallen into a mine shaft. Casey cautiously felt for the wall of rock that likely surrounded them, but hit nothing but air. Adrenaline sparked in her chest. They couldn't have hit bottom and survived. Impossible. Besides, hadn't all these old shafts flooded decades ago? She'd read that in her research. Surviving a fall into one of the mine shafts in the area was highly improbable.

"I think we're on some sort of platform." At least Stark had fallen beside her. "Not possible." He had to be mistaken. Still, if not a platform, what had broken their fall? "These old mine shafts are hundreds of feet deep and there are no ledges or platforms. The miners were hoisted up and down." She tried to remember if she had seen anything besides sandy dirt and scrub before falling. Nothing came to mind. The rush to escape their captor had happened too fast.

Her fingers tightened into balls of frustration. The urge to move—to investigate her surroundings—was almost overwhelming. But she wanted to stay alive more. Due consideration was needed before taking any action.

"We fell maybe eight or ten feet," Stark said. "Not that far but whatever we hit isn't stable."

She'd been too busy trying to grab on to something to notice. Admittedly she was still a little shaky from the blow to her head. Good thing Stark had been paying attention. That said, the scenario of their landing didn't add up.

"If you're correct in your calculations, we can't be in a shaft unless..." Holy-moly. Unless some environmentally challenged imbecile had used this shaft for dumping and part of the junk tossed inside had gotten wedged at this point. Her heart stumbled. If whatever had stopped their fall moved... Stark had said it was unstable. Unstable meant movement. Her heart quickened its pace.

"You should've let go of me when I told you to," she complained. Now look at the quandary they were in. This temporary reprieve was just that—*temporary*. Better to die hard and fast than to be forced to contemplate it for a few minutes.

"That's right," he grumped back at her. "This is definitely all my fault. It had nothing to do with the nimrod dancing on my hand. If you'll recall, I was managing to hang on until he showed up."

"Timing, Stark. You should have dropped me minutes before that and you would've had ample time to climb out and crack the guy's skull." She was right. He was wrong. Enough said about that. Of course if this ledge or garbage or whatever hadn't broken her fall she would be dead anyway. At least with one of them above ground their odds of getting out of this mess would have greatly increased. That was strategic thinking. Now they were both screwed. If this chunk of whatever moved and falling hundreds of feet didn't get them, the arsenic and lead-laced water surely would.

Her uncle would not be happy. Lucas wouldn't be either.

"Let's say this isn't one of those deep mine shafts," Stark suggested with admirable optimism. "We could, presumably, move around without that much risk."

Big fat if. There was no way to be certain except to give it a test. Casey reached out again, this time daring to lift her upper body from whatever they were lying on. She stretched until her fingers hit a wall. She scraped at it, then rubbed the tips together.

Dirt.

The three hundred or so mine shafts in the area had walls of stone. She'd done thorough research on the area. Evidently Stark had not. Anticipation forced her heart to pump harder. The dirt was a good sign. "You could be right." It was a gamble but they couldn't just lounge here as if they were dead already.

Something scurried across her leg. Casey clamped her jaws shut to hold back the instinctive squeal.

Rats.

An epiphany dawned and a smile tugged at her lips. Even rats needed to climb out of their holes from time to time. How far up or down did rats crawl? Another question contradicting their positive analysis of the situation zinged her. If they were only eight or ten feet down, lying atop a garbage heap, why couldn't she see the stars above them?

Her smile resurrected and widened to a grin. They'd fallen hard and fast, then the momentum had slowed because the opening had narrowed as they slid along at an angle until they hit this ledge or whatever. She touched her chin where it had scrubbed the dirt. Oh yeah, she remembered now. She'd been a little rattled after the fall, but she was on her mental toes now.

Casey scooted forward a bit and reached above her head. The heap beneath her groaned and stirred.

"Whoa. What're you doing?" Stark grabbed her arm. "Take it easy."

"Climbing out." Ignoring him and the

way his touch sent a streak of electricity along her skin, she cautiously moved up onto her hands and knees. The mound beneath her shifted slightly a second time. She froze.

Stark froze, too. He didn't even yell at her, though he definitely muttered something unintelligible.

When Casey's pulse rate slowed to a more reasonable level, she started again. One hand forward, then one knee. Repeat. Pausing after each repeat to check the area in front of her as best she could in the dark, she slowly but surely moved beyond the slight angle that had blocked her view of the sky.

Stars spread across the inky night sky like silver rhinestones on a black satin dress. "You were right," she called over her shoulder. "We're down about eight feet, maybe a little more." Still taking care, she eased into a standing position. The opening of the hole was another four or five feet above her head. Not close enough.

Stark moved up beside her. "Feels pretty steady here."

Nothing had shifted since the initial

movements. A few minutes more of that good fortune and they could be out of here. She turned to Stark. "You think you can hold my weight?"

He turned his face toward hers. She couldn't read his eyes with nothing more than the starlight. "I think I've already established that."

"I guess you did." She scooted behind him and grabbed his shoulders with both hands. She felt his muscles bunch beneath her touch. Understandable. She ached all over. She imagined he did as well. Couldn't have anything to do with that crazy mingling of heat she experienced whenever they touched.

Casey took a breath and plunged upward, scaling his backside like a monkey. "Don't look up," she warned as she settled first one foot, then the other on his shoulders. She thanked God for the wide-bottomed, swishy skirt which made maneuvering a whole lot easier. So long as he didn't look up and get an eyeful of her half-naked bottom. Skimpy undies could be a nuisance at times.

She rose to her full height and her head

and shoulders broke into the night air. *Freedom.* She scanned the terrain, then listened for a full ten seconds. Clear. No guys wearing sweatshirts. No truck and no gunfire. Now all she needed was something to grab on to. Casey scratched at the ground beyond the boards, but she couldn't reach anything that would give her the necessary leverage.

"Can you push me a little higher?" Just a few more inches would do it.

His right hand touched her heel. Holding on to the edges of the boards, she lifted that foot so his palm and fingers could cradle it. The left was trickier. She swayed, but Stark steadied her as he lifted her.

And she was out of the hole up to her thighs.

She grabbed two handfuls of scrub and directed all her energy into hauling her lower body up. Her skirt caught on the splintered boards; she yanked it loose, ripping the delicate fabric at the hem.

Casey scrambled onto all fours, pressed her cheek to the ground and gave silent thanks. She did a one-eighty and peered down at Stark. "I made it."

"I never had a doubt."

He sounded chipper enough but he had to be wondering what she would do next. Man oh man, his head was a good four or five feet below her reach. Even with him extending his arms as far as possible she wouldn't be able to get a hold on him. Not to mention she would need leverage up here to give him any assistance. Hanging her upper body over the edge wouldn't work.

"You still have that tire iron?" The surrounding area appeared to be clear at the moment, but trouble could step from behind one of the ruins at any time. A weapon might come in handy. She'd dropped the switchblade along with the flashlight.

"Here you go."

The tire iron appeared in front of her. She stretched down into the hole as far as she dared and grabbed the tip of it. Placing it close by just in case, she shifted her attention back to Stark and how the heck she was going to help him. The hole was too wide for him to use his arms or his legs against the side walls to climb upward.

"Take off your belt." It might not be long

enough but it could work. She had to try all options.

The hiss of leather against cotton signaled he was complying with her request. She shivered. It was cold. Not to mention her adrenaline had run rampant and it was now receding. Shivers were to be expected.

Stark tossed the belt upward; she snagged it on the first attempt. After looping it around her wrist, she pushed the tail end through the buckle, then pulled it tight.

Casey dangled the end down to him and braced herself. "Let's give it a try."

"You won't be able to handle my weight." All traces of optimism had vanished.

"We won't know until we try." Truth was, she wasn't all that optimistic herself. Her arm and head were over the edge. She was strong but not nearly that strong. Still, she had to try.

Stark shook his head. "Walk back to town and get help. I'll chill out here."

Funny. "We've had this conversation before, Stark. Now grab hold of the belt."

"Just don't fall back in here." He reached up and wrapped the end of the belt around one hand. "Here goes nothing."

Casey rolled her eyes. If she were a guy they wouldn't be having this conversation.

Stark bent one knee upward and dug the toe of his boot into the dirt wall. When he was satisfied that he had a toehold, he looked up at her. "You set?"

"Climb already."

The belt tightened on her wrist. Casey grabbed on with her other hand and dug her elbows into the ground. His weight dragged against hers and she slid forward. A yelp ripped out of her before she could stop it.

He let go of the belt.

A crash echoed inside the hole.

A scream trapped in her throat, Casey peered down at him. He was okay. Thank God.

He turned his face up to hers. "Go for help. This isn't going to work."

What was wrong with this guy? She was no quitter. Casey looked around again and found a large clump of scrub brush a couple feet away. But there was nothing near enough to help. Wait. There might be stuff in the old ruins.

"I'll be back." She grabbed the tire iron

and headed for the nearest dilapidated building.

She couldn't move as quickly as she would have liked for fear of falling into another unmarked hazard. The mine shafts were all supposed to be marked. Supposed to be evidently didn't always pan out.

An old bucket. A bench. Couple of large stones. Nothing useful. That she could carry anyway.

Casey scrubbed the back of her hand over her forehead. What now? Every minute he was down there was a risk. Fernandez's goons could show up to ensure their loose ends were tied up. The heap holding Stark could give way. She wasn't adequately prepared.

Then an idea occurred to her.

Enthusiasm recharging, she picked her way back to the hole where she'd left Stark and dropped to her knees. She leaned forward. "Take off your jeans."

A considerable expanse of startled silence lapsed. Then, "Is that a pickup line?"

"Ha ha." He was a comedian. "Now take off your pants and toss 'em up here."

"You have a new plan?" He didn't bother concealing the skepticism in his voice.

"Just trust me, Stark," she advised, her impatience flashing like a neon sign.

"Trust you?" One of those deep, sexy—okay, she'd said it, *sexy*—laughs echoed from below. "Why not? I've trusted you this far, I guess."

"Fine. Just hurry up. It's cold up here." She shivered, the chill creeping all the way to her bones.

He reached for his fly and glanced up. "Do you have to watch?"

Casey sat back, her arms hugged around her to keep the cold at bay. She should have walked back to town. Maybe she would have been there by now. Instead she was freezing out here in the desert while some guy she'd just met shucked his pants. A guy who had trespassed into her mission.

The jeans landed on the ground in front of her. Good shot. She picked them up and, despite the circumstances, checked the brand. "Pricey." Now if the construction would just take the stress of what she was about to do.

After tossing the end of one leg down

to him, she wrapped herself around the bigger scrub bush and coiled the hem end of the second leg in her fists. Casey had no idea how deep the roots of these Mexican shrubs went, but any extra leverage would be useful.

"Ready?" he called out.

"As I'll ever be." That statement was far too true.

This was it. There were no other options, except walking out of here alone. Stranger or not, competition or not, Casey didn't want to leave Stark out here.

Was she really that afraid of being alone? Lately it sure as heck seemed so.

Stop with the ridiculous questions. Her mom had planted that idea in her head and obviously it had taken root. *Stay on this course and you're going to end up alone like your uncle Thomas.* That was ridiculous. Her parents had been married for thirty years. 'Course they had married before her father joined the Agency. And what about Lucas? He had Victoria. Her mom was overreacting just because she wanted grandchildren and Casey had no siblings.

The slack wrenched out of the jeans. Casey closed her eyes and concentrated on holding her ground. One, two, three seconds passed with the strain mounting fast.

"Come on, come on," she muttered. *Hold on just a little longer.*

The bush gave a little. Casey's eyes snapped open. "Hurry, Stark!"

She couldn't hold out much longer. He had to make it fast. She dug her heels into the dirt for more leverage.

His head, then his shoulders appeared. Then his upper body was up and out.

Casey resisted the urge to relax. Not until he was all the way out.

One long, bare leg—save for the fancy boot—swung up onto the ground. Then the other. He rolled away from the hole but didn't get up.

Casey uncoiled herself from the bush and got to her feet. A frown wrinkled her forehead. Was he hurt?

She walked closer. "You okay, Stark?" He wore paisley boxers. She laughed. Hadn't meant to, but once she started she couldn't stop.

He stared at her until she stopped. When she did, he said in a very pointed tone, "I'm fine. But I'd rather not get up until I have my pants."

Casey burst into laughter again. She couldn't help it. Maybe she was giddy with relief or just plain hysterical. Either way Stark wasn't amused.

Stark rolled onto his side and pushed up in a move smooth enough to impress even her. He wrenched off one boot, then the other and tossed them aside. He stalked up to her, sporting socked feet and those unexpected paisley boxers, bent down and claimed his jeans. He shook the dust off and pulled them on, all without taking his eyes off hers. If she hadn't been so busy staring at him she might have had the presence of mind to hand him the jeans.

When he'd fastened the fly, she gestured toward the hole. "I think your belt's over there somewhere."

Casey gave him time to get his boots and belt in order before confessing, "You can head straight back to town if you want but I'm planning on paying Fernandez a little visit." Maybe get the info he'd promised. "His place is on the way."

Stark held up the tire iron. "You think you'll need more than this?"

This part was going to be complicated. "I came here to do a job. I'm not leaving until it's done." She folded her arms over her chest, more from the cold than as a display of determination. But she was determined. This was her plan. She didn't need his approval or his cooperation. Be that as it may, some clue as to what he had in mind could prove useful.

"Well." He dropped the tire iron to his side. "I have the same dilemma." He braced his hands on his hips. "I suppose it would be a conflict of interest to work together toward that common goal. Never mind that I've proven my reliability and trustworthiness under considerably dicey conditions."

Was he proposing they help each other? Or was this a trick of some sort? What if their employers were mortal enemies? This could get complicated fast. "I'd have to know who you're working for first."

He held out his hands, palms up. "That's one thing I can't give you."

Casey's jaw dropped. That was ridiculous. "You want to work together but you can't tell me who sent you?" Totally unacceptable.

"All right." He put his hands on his lean hips. "Tell me who you're working for and I'll do the same."

Her shoulders tensed. Classified, Lucas had said. "Sorry." They were at an impasse. "I can't do that. But," she added quickly, "only because I'm under strict orders from my employer. Not because the information is relevant to you." All true. Not that she owed him an explanation.

Stark glanced over his shoulder and considered the lay of the land in the direction of the road then settled his attention back on her. He shrugged. "Well, we're headed the same way."

"We are." An entirely exaggerated awareness of him had her pulse speeding up again.

"No reason we can't walk together," he suggested.

"No reason at all," she allowed.

He gestured in the direction they'd come

in a dead run from the bad guy. "Ladies first."

Shoulders squared, she stalked past him. He caught up with her and draped his jacket over her shoulders, all without missing a step.

"You look cold."

She stopped and glared at him. "I'm fine." She offered his jacket back to him.

Instead of grabbing it, he took his time rolling down the sleeves of his shirt, first one, then the other. "It's a long walk back to Fernandez's place. It's pretty cold out here."

Casey exhaled a lungful of frustration. "Fine. Fine. Fine." She dragged on the jacket, sliding her arms into the too-long sleeves. His scent immediately invaded her nostrils… His body heat still warmed the inside of the jacket.

Dear God! What was wrong with her?

She marched forward, ignoring the man and the assault on her senses.

He fell into step beside her. "Thanks for rescuing me back there."

"Not a problem."

"Nice panties, by the way."

She kept walking. He was lucky. Really lucky she didn't have a gun in her hand.

If he survived until daylight he would be even luckier.

Chapter Six

Outside, Paulo Fernandez's home and landscape remained as rustic as when he'd purchased the abandoned mining hacienda. But inside, he'd clearly spent extravagantly to create a retreat suitable for a royal. Too bad he was anything but royal.

The two goofballs who had been charged with disposing of Casey and Stark were evidently groveling for forgiveness. Casey watched through a window near the front of the house as the two cowered in the center of the great room while Fernandez paced back and forth across the stone floor ranting and waving his arms like a dictator. There seemed to be little pleasure in paradise. If those two thought Fernandez was giving them a hard time, just wait until Casey got her turn. She hadn't looked forward to getting even this much since her last field assignment for the Agency.

Irritation rumbled in her belly at the idea that she'd been assigned to a desk for the last six months. Yeah, she'd almost taken a bullet a few times—three to be exact—in her two years of field service prior to that. The last time didn't count in her opinion since the bullet had scarcely grazed its target. But the powers that be had labeled her reckless.

Was it her fault the hostage had gotten injured during retrieval? Not at all. The guy had been a spoiled brat of a prince who hadn't grown up in twenty-five years. He should have followed her orders. Then there wouldn't have been an *almost* international incident. And he wouldn't have needed a Band-Aid for the scrape he'd suffered.

Casey kicked the frustrating thoughts aside. Maybe this vacation—that was what her superiors at the Agency thought she was doing—would demonstrate that she was more than capable of showing restraint and caution. She hadn't killed or even injured anyone yet.

"When he's finished chewing them out," Stark whispered, the sound so close to her ear she nearly jumped out of her skin, "maybe he'll throw them out and the odds will be more in our favor."

Casey eased back from the window, needing to put some space between her and Stark since, for some reason, she seemed to have an issue controlling her physical reaction to his voice. There was no landscape lighting, so no fear of them being seen outside the restored soaring windows. Fernandez hadn't bothered with window coverings anywhere on the first floor. She imagined that he assumed the dirty build-up on the glass would do the trick.

"Especially after we disable them and take their weapons," she said in response to Stark's suggestion.

Stark raised an eyebrow at her strategy, drawing her attention to his unusual green eyes for the hundredth time. She disliked immensely that she was so taken with the color.

"Subduing Fernandez would likely garner their compliance," he argued. "In light of their less than stellar performance so far I'd recommend something less than an excessive show of force. Get in, get out with the least amount of resistance."

"They have guns, Stark." Did he have to argue with her every approach? If this was his idea of teamwork, she was out.

"That would be my point." He shifted his attention back to the drama inside. "We're not armed and Fernandez appears not to carry a weapon, making for a more level playing field."

He probably viewed busting in as a bad idea, too.

"Waiting until Fernandez calls it a night will provide the optimum opportunity," he went on. "His underlings will retire to their quarters and we'll have the least interference."

Casey knew it. Stark would take the most conservative approach. Every step they had made together so far had teemed with caution. They hadn't gotten twenty yards in this direction before he'd stopped and insisted on going back to search the area around the hole they'd fallen in for the weapon he'd taken from the bad guy. It hadn't mattered that she explained repeatedly that she had not seen the weapon while trying to figure out a way to get him out of said hole. That proved, without a doubt, that he did not trust her. How were they supposed to work together if he didn't trust her?

When they had finally reached Fernandez's place, they had searched the small outbuilding before advancing to the main house. The outbuilding seemed deserted and no weapons had been lying around, but it was obvious that the building served as a bunkhouse for Fernandez's pals. A man like him would never share a roof with the help.

"Waiting," Casey countered. "That's your plan?"

"You're suggesting that yours is better?" He waved the tire iron in her face, the rusty weapon made significantly less threatening by the dim glow from the window. "Since we're so well prepared and all."

"We compromise." Casey turned the notion over in her head. "We lay in wait in the bunkhouse and surprise his men. Put them out of commission, then we'll have the advantage of no distractions and we'll be armed. Convincing Fernandez to talk will be a breeze." Made perfect sense to her, but then she was a highly trained agent.

Stark deliberated for long enough to make her want to shake him. She wasn't going to like his response. Exasperation roiled in her gut. This was exactly why she preferred working without a partner. Far too much energy was expended on talk rather than action.

"Must the last word always belong to you?"

She'd expected a flat-out no or maybe a counter plan. Definitely not such a personal question. No, not a question. He'd made a statement disguised as a question. An outright accusation. "Is that a yes?" They were wasting time. Since Fernandez was no longer pacing she had to assume the discussion inside was winding down.

"Why not?" Stark directed his attention back to the scene inside the house.

Would it have been so difficult to respond with a simple yes? She checked the status of those inside one last time before moving away from the window. When she was clear, she pushed upright and hustled to the outbuilding they had decided was a bunkhouse. Stark followed close behind her.

Casey had never worked with a P.I. before. If they were all this conservative she didn't see how they ever completed a mission successfully.

The bunkhouse was unlocked. In fact, there wasn't a lock at all. Casey supposed Fernandez's security or cleanup detail, whatever those two called themselves, weren't concerned with their own personal safety. Made Casey's job a whole lot easier. The door's hinges creaked with age and neglect, making her cringe though she knew the noise was coming. The smell of overloaded ashtrays and sweaty socks wasn't any more aromatic now than it had been the first time she'd entered.

Like the landscape, the interior of the one-room structure was rustic and desolate. Light beyond that of the moon filtering in the windows was not required to survey the sparsely furnished space. Wood floors and walls that had been around several decades. Windows with no glass, just small rectangles cut out of the walls. A couple beat-up iron beds with shabby blankets covering the mattresses. The chest of drawers loaded with unwashed clothes had been searched and there was nothing on the wobbly table other than a couple empty beer bottles. A single bare bulb dangled over the table and its accompanying woven bottom chairs. A rusty fridge held more beer. The place was a real dump.

Casey took a position at one of the windows facing the back of the main house. Stark stayed near the door. She needed a weapon. They'd checked under the scrawny mattresses already as well as every other nook and cranny in the joint. There was no place else to look.

The beer bottles. She smiled and moved as soundlessly as possible to the table. One in each hand, she resumed her position at the window just in time to watch the two *hombres* swagger from the back of the main house. She drew back but there was no worry. The men were too busy arguing about who screwed up to look, even if they had been able to see her in the dark.

She glanced toward Stark; he had faded

into the shadows on the other side of the door. Doing the same, she flattened against the wall, putting the chest of drawers between her and the door.

The hinges whined as the back door opened. Their booted footsteps echoed loudly as the two men stamped into the room, still growling at each other.

Casey held her breath.

The man in the gray sweatshirt dragged out a chair, the legs scraping across the wood floor, and collapsed into it. She braced for him to yank at the chain, turning on the overhead light but he didn't. Anger lit beneath her breastbone. This was the idiot who'd chased them through a literal mine field.

Guy Two ranted in Spanish, basically reenacting the scene with their boss, as he slammed the door. He blamed his partner for not putting a bullet in Casey's and Stark's heads sooner. He opened the fridge door. A dim burst of light pooled around him. Casey held absolutely still, the blood roaring in her ears. The faint glow didn't reach her or Stark's position.

The big-mouthed goon slammed the

fridge door, still blustering as if he were the *jefe* around here. According to him, now there was no way to say for sure until daylight if Casey and Stark had fallen into a mine shaft or one of the *de basura* holes.

She had thought as much. The hole hadn't been a mine shaft. It had been a hole for illegally disposing of garbage.

In her peripheral vision she saw Stark make his move. The smug guy standing crumpled to the floor when hit with the tire iron. His sweatshirt-sporting friend shot up, his chair toppling over. Casey bolted forward and whacked him on the head with the beer bottle in her right hand. Glass shattered on the floor. When he turned and made a dive at her, his gun already palmed, she gave him another smack with the one in her left. He crashed the same way his *amigo* had.

Casey tugged the 9mm from the guy closest to her and tucked it into the waistband of her skirt at the small of her back. Her mind already two steps ahead, she shuffled through the drawers of the chest until she had four shirts to use in securing the buttwads on the floor. She pitched two Stark's way.

Working swiftly, they didn't speak until they tied the goons' hands behind their backs, then secured the makeshift tether to their bound ankles. Getting loose wouldn't be so easy. Socks stuffed in their mouths would ensure they didn't sound an alarm for their boss.

Stark placed his hand on her shoulder. She looked up at him, hoping he didn't notice the quiver his touch had evoked. Why the heck did she keep doing that? "Slow and quiet," he warned. "We want him alive and talking."

Maybe it shouldn't have, but his cautionary advice ticked her off. She hadn't planned to go in guns-a-blazing. He sounded like her superiors at the Agency. "Got it."

She shrugged off his touch and moved to the door. She wasn't reckless; she was bold...brave...unflinching. If she gave off that vibe, what of it? She was glad. She wasn't weak, so why pretend?

The wind had picked up outside. Raising her hand to her face, Casey protected her eyes from the sand that might be flying around. She and Stark reached the main house without incident. Hopefully that meant Fernandez had either retired for the evening or wasn't near any of the windows that faced the back of his property.

At the same window where they'd been before, Casey carefully peeked inside. Fernandez had slumped into a large wing chair with a tall glass. Judging by the small amount of golden liquid that remained, he was on his way to exceedingly relaxed.

Tequila could steal the roar from a lion. It had helped many find the floor.

Casey considered their options and decided that the straightforward approach would be the most efficient method of achieving their goal. She crouched down below the window and waited for Stark to join her.

"I'm guessing the back door was left unlocked."

Stark nodded, to her surprise. "If he hears us, he'll think it's one of them." He jerked his head toward the bunkhouse.

True. "He certainly won't be expecting us." The sweetest kind of revenge. She was going to enjoy this, as long as Stark didn't get in her way.

Casey stayed down until she was clear of the window. A few seconds were required to reach the back of the house. She flattened against the wall and listened. The silence bugged her a little. Too bad Fernandez wasn't watching a favorite movie or playing a few tunes. Going for a quiet entrance could backfire if the floor creaked or she bumped into something. The rooms at the back of the house were dark. The smarter move would be to go in loud, like the *locos* out in the bunkhouse.

Stark faced her from the opposite side of the rear entrance. Casey held up one finger, then two. He was braced to move on three. She didn't bother with three. She barged through the door, too fast for Stark to snatch her back.

The back door led straight into the kitchen. She stamped into the wide entry hall that appeared to connect the kitchen to the front rooms. She took a position next to a towering cabinet with glass doors. Behind the glass were all manner of exquisite art pieces. At least the lying scumbag had decent taste.

The hall was wide and dimly lit by the light valiantly stretching across the floor from the front room where Fernandez had been lounging.

"What the hell do you want now?" Fernandez howled. "I told you to get out!"

Stoneware crashed on the floor of the kitchen. Stark. Casey grinned. He got it. Her new partner was luring the prey from his safety zone.

"If you broke anything important," Fernandez promised, the sound of his voice growing nearer, "I will make you eat it and laugh as you bleed to death." Obviously he saw using English with his thugs at moments like this as a way to prove his superiority.

One step...two... He passed right in front of her position and she stepped out to press the muzzle of the borrowed 9mm to his temple. "Maybe you'll be the one bleeding to death." She sighed with all the drama she could muster. "Afraid I couldn't lose my tracker."

Stark flipped on the overhead light, the

9mm he'd snagged zeroed in on Fernandez's head.

"I guess you'll just have to deal with it," Casey said with a nudge of the muzzle.

Fernandez said nothing for a moment, his lips twisted in anger. "My order was to tell you nothing."

"Who gave the order?" Stark demanded before Casey could. He took a menacing step toward Fernandez. She had to admit that he looked plenty threatening.

"I cannot say!" Fernandez shook his head frantically. "She will kill me!"

"No problem," Casey offered generously. Her grip tightened on the weapon and she widened her stance. "I'll just put you out of your misery now and you can stop worrying about that."

"No. Wait."

Casey tossed Stark a look that loudly transmitted her exasperation. His announcement startled her almost as much as it irritated her. Fernandez, on the other hand, sagged with relief.

"Get the broken platter," Stark ordered.

Casey smiled. Oh, he had a twisted side

she hadn't expected. "This should be interesting."

She backed toward the kitchen, a bead held steady on her target even as she moved past Stark's position.

In the kitchen she flipped on a light and shoved her weapon into the waistband of her damaged skirt. While she squatted down and gathered a few choice pieces of pottery, she heard Stark ushering Fernandez into a chair. When she returned to the hall, a chair had been placed in the center of the rectangular space and Fernandez was secured there. His crisp white shirt served as a tether. Smart move to stay in the hall away from the windows of the other rooms since there were no window coverings. If either of the goofballs got loose, she and Stark wouldn't be open targets.

"Feed him," Stark said without sparing her a glance.

Casey wouldn't have liked his heavy-handedness if she weren't enjoying this so much. She strolled over to Fernandez and offered a sizeable chunk of what used to be a serving platter. The pattern suggested a local artisan. This was going to be a waste of good stoneware. Fernandez drew his face away from her, his mouth clamped shut.

Stark pressed the barrel of his weapon to Fernandez's forehead. "Open your mouth."

Leaning back far enough to topple over, Fernandez shook his head adamantly.

Casey rolled her eyes. "Just shoot him. I'm bored with the whole subject."

Stark shrugged. "Whatever you say."

"Wait!" Fernandez looked from Casey to Stark and back. "If I tell you and she finds out, she will—"

"You said that already." Casey really was getting bored.

Fernandez heaved a labored breath. "The person you're looking for lives in Acapulco." He shook his head as he spouted off the address. "She is blonde. Like you," he said with a toss of his head toward Casey. "She works as a dancer and choreographer at a club called Delicia. Her name is Alayna. She can tell you anything you want to know about this man you call Keaton." Fernandez made eye contact with Casey. "Believe me when I say to you that she knows the answers you seek."

"We need a last name." What good was a first name? Acapulco was a big city. Casey rolled her eyes. Did he think they were stupid enough to let him off with nothing more than that? She could just imagine what kind of place Delicia was. The name itself meant pleasure.

"She has no last name," Fernandez explained with another of those annoying half laughs. "Not that anyone knows, I assure you. However, you must trust me when I say that you will have no trouble finding her. Everyone knows Alayna."

"You could be lying as easily as telling the truth," Stark countered, the weapon creasing Fernandez's forehead once more. "Give me one good reason I should trust you after you tried to kill us."

Oddly, Fernandez smiled but it lacked his usual confidence. "That is always the case in this sort of business, Señor Stark. Surely you have encountered this tedious detail before."

Out of patience, Casey drew the weapon from her waistband and poked Fernandez in the head just for the fun of it. "So you don't have a problem with our coming back here to settle the score if you're lying, right?"

Fernandez shook his head again. "Ah, *chiquita,* but I will not be here if you return."

Uncertainty trickled into her veins. There was something way off with this guy. Besides the fact that he was a lying, cheating, thieving piece of subhuman slime.

"You see," Fernandez explained, staring directly into Casey's eyes, "when she learns what I have done, she will kill me. As for your one good reason to trust me after recent events—" he shrugged one shoulder "—what other choice do you have?"

He was right about that. "I wouldn't worry about her if I were you," Casey pointed out. "Your problem is me." She remembered Stark a second too late. "And him." So much for being a team player. Chancing a glance in his direction was out of the question. "If you're lying, we will hunt you down and make you wish you'd chosen more wisely."

"No matter where you hide," Stark added with a smile that was anything but pleasant.

Fernandez laughed long and loudly, dragging Casey's full attention back to him. "I will have no reason to fear the two of you if you find her." He shook his head, his eyes wild with something like hysteria.

"You underestimate us, sir," Stark said, the same fury smoldering in his voice that was currently coming to a hard boil inside Casey. "You should be very afraid."

"What is there to fear from the dead?" Fernandez proposed. "If you find her, you will not live to share her secrets with anyone."

Chapter Seven

October 12, 2:45 a.m.

"We'll take the truck." Levi strode in that direction as he spoke. He'd checked and the gas gauge was close to full, unlike the other vehicle which had less than half a tank. The sooner they were out of here, the better he would feel. No matter that they had taken all three of the men's cell phones and there was no house phone, he couldn't count on Fernandez's word that a call wouldn't be made as soon as one or all were loose.

"I'll get the truck," Casey said, rushing ahead of him. "Disable the Jeep. Fernandez may have another set of keys we don't know about."

Changing directions, Levi agreed, "Good idea." The lady continued to impress him. Good thing the Jeep was an older model because he was no mechanic. Since most of his college buddies had driven older vehicles and pranks were often a rite of passage, Levi knew exactly how to do this and no tools were needed. He ripped out the plug wires and the coil wire to the distributor cap, just to make it a little more complicated. Either one would have done the trick. Getting parts at this hour wouldn't be easy, particularly out here.

He tossed the wires into the bed of the truck and started to climb into the driver's seat. Casey had already taken that position.

"I'll drive."

He gave her a nod and hustled around to the other side. "Where we headed?"

"Back to the hotel." She shoved the gearshift into Drive and roared down the dirt road. "I'll grab my stuff." She pointed to the bench seat where her purse sat between them. "They went through my bag but everything seems to be there, including my credit cards."

Levi was about to suggest they didn't leave a paper trail by using credit cards when she interrupted the thought with,

"I always carry plastic under a couple of aliases in case I need them."

Who was this chick? "I'm not asking you to name your client," he said as the truck bounced out onto the main road, "but are you a contractor, P.I. or what?"

"What difference does it make?"

"Maybe none." He braced against his door as she floored the accelerator and sent the old pickup charging forward. "I'm more curious than anything."

"Well." She exhaled a big breath. "This mission isn't for my employer. It's for a… friend. Technically I'm on vacation."

Sounded familiar. "That's funny, so am I."

She sent him a lingering, sideways glance. Too bad there wasn't enough light to get some idea what she was thinking. He didn't have to wonder long.

"That is funny."

Ah, suspicion. Just what he needed to sustain her cooperation. "What's the plan?" Letting her think she had the lead might alleviate the tension along with some of her suspicions.

Another of those long looks arrowed his

way. "You're asking me?" She focused on the road a second or two, then asked, "Did you have something in mind?"

"I'm at the same hotel as you, by the way," he offered, sidestepping her question. In reality, there was only one strategy— find this Alayna and get some answers— but he supposed there were a number of ways one could go about that step.

"Good. We can get our stuff and get out of Pozos before Fernandez sends his pals this way."

That was assuming those pals hadn't cleared out their stuff at the hotel. Levi doubted they'd had the opportunity but there could be others working for Fernandez.

With Casey focused on driving, Levi used the opportunity to study her. Not that he could make out the finer details in the dark, but he focused on those he already knew better than he should.

Not good, Levi. She was the competition on this mission. Their alliance might be in place for only as long as it took to attain the information on Keaton. There was no way just yet to guess how things would go down from there. If he was lucky, he would have some measure of her ultimate intent before then.

His primary mission, other than to gain the information, was to protect Victoria's identity. Whatever else happened, he had to keep her secret safe.

THE VILLAGE OF POZOS WAS tucked in for the night as Casey parked the truck on the street near the entrance of their hotel. The lack of street lamps to chase away the shadows would serve them well. The fewer who witnessed their movements the better.

"The less time we spend here," he recommended as she opened the driver's side door, "the less likely we are to run into trouble."

"Absolutely."

She was out of the truck and headed for the entrance by the time his feet hit the cobblestone street. As usual, he followed her path. That was apparently going to be the MO for this team. He watched her softly curved hips sway and decided following wasn't such a hardship.

The lobby was as silent as this ghost

town had been just a few years back. The main entry doors as well as the windows were open, allowing the night breeze to play with the drapes and the wind chimes. The otherwise quiet rattled Levi's nerves. Or maybe it was the idea that they'd come back here knowing time was their enemy.

It was four hours minimum to Acapulco. A lot could happen in four hours, like Fernandez sending a warning to this Alayna they needed to find. Somehow Levi believed him when he said he was afraid of her. Maybe Fernandez would take off, as he'd said, allowing him a head start before Alayna learned of his treachery.

"Meet you at the truck in five minutes," Casey whispered when they reached the second-floor landing.

Levi was on this floor, too, but on the opposite end of the building. He'd checked into the mystery woman who'd been asking questions about Keaton as soon as he'd learned of her from Fernandez. Casey had arrived in a rental car and was in room four. She was American and blonde. That was the extent of the available info a dozen hours ago.

He didn't know much more about her now…which was exactly why splitting up was a bad idea. "We should stick together." She stared at him like he'd lost his mind. "Just in case."

Her gaze narrowed. "Sure. Yeah. Good idea." She gave him her back and hurried along the corridor.

She'd seen right through that one. He probably would've been disappointed if she hadn't. She'd been damned sharp so far.

She dug the key to her room from the funky bag she carried. Really worn leather with fringe on the flap that closed over the bag's zipper. Cute, kind of.

"Gimme ninety seconds."

"I'll be right here." Levi leaned against the open door frame so he could keep an eye on the hall outside the room. Casey dashed around the room snatching up discarded clothes. She pulled out the bottom drawer of the night table next to her bed and removed a 9mm. Lifting her skirt, she removed a thigh holster before tucking them both into her bag, then she moved to the desk.

If she could pull her stuff together in ninety seconds he would really be impressed. In his experience, women generally had their stuff strewn all over a place like they were marking their territory. He, on the other hand, would grab his carry-on bag and be good to go. And men were the ones accused of marking their territory. Not the case at all when it came to living space.

"I'm ready. Where's your room?"

Startled from his men-travel-light musings, he straightened from the door and glanced around the room. "You got everything?"

"Got it. Now which room is yours?" she asked while he was still dawdling there trying to decide whether he could believe his eyes and ears.

He hitched a thumb. "One."

She sidled past him and out the door. "What're we waiting for? Let's get a move on."

Levi kicked himself into gear and gained a lead on her. His room was on the other end of the corridor past the main staircase. He fished the key from his pocket and opened the door. While he crossed the room and snagged his still packed bag, she waited at the door just as he'd done at her room.

One last, quick survey and he was done.

"Ready." He approached the door, expecting her to step aside.

"You don't have access to the verandah." She shrugged. "Too bad. You missed an awesome view. Who booked your room?"

He wasn't falling for that one. "We shouldn't risk waking anyone." The longer they stood around here talking the greater the possibility.

She turned and sauntered to the staircase, boosting the sass in her step by at least ten degrees. Every single one of those degrees raised his internal thermostat. This lady was going to be extremely difficult to handle and they were only getting started.

Levi reached the truck first so he claimed the driver's seat. No offense to her driving skill, but he preferred driving versus riding with a virtual stranger.

He checked the back and beneath the seat to see that all was in order. The street was still dark and empty. If luck remained on

their side, they might survive this some-
what unorthodox alliance.

Maybe the next four and a half to five
hours on the road with nothing to do but
chat or ride in silence would reveal more
about this mystery lady. He needed a lot
more to fully appraise his position. She
had already shown that getting information wasn't going to be easy.

Five minutes passed with nothing but
that silence he'd figured he was in for and
then out of the blue she started to talk. "It'll
be close to daylight by the time we get to
Acapulco." She dug around in her bag. "We
can find a hotel near the club and shower
and change. If she's a nightclub dancer
she's probably not an early riser. That'll
work to our benefit, assuming she doesn't
get word we're headed her way and disappear. We'll have some time to get the lay
of the land. Develop a feasible plan."

Total silence, then all that. Wow. His
response to her in-depth assessment went
by the wayside as she leaned forward and
closely inspected the dash. "What're you
looking for?" The interior lights in this old
pickup were worthless. That aside, he could

make out the shape of her derriere quite well in the moonlight.

"A place to plug in my cell charger. I'm hoping I'll have service when we get closer to the city."

"You're out of luck, I think." He doubted this old thing had a cigarette lighter, much less a car charger outlet.

She blew out a disgusted breath and plopped back in the seat. "That's just great. I guess it'll wait until we get a room."

Levi took a mental pause. "*A* room."

She looked at him. He didn't have to turn his head to see; he could feel the glare as surely as if the noonday sun was glinting against the windows.

"Do you really believe I'm going to let you out of my sight with the information we have now?" She faced forward. "Not happening, *partner.*"

Once again, not exactly a hardship. Generally he was the one doing the asking when it came to sharing a room with the opposite sex. Under considerably different circumstances, of course.

"We're partners now, are we?" To his

way of thinking partners was a step up from working together.

"Don't make too much of it, Stark." She finger combed her hair. "It's only out of necessity."

"Naturally." Levi propped a smile in place. "Our options were limited."

"Exactly," she agreed. "I'm in enough trouble at work already. I have no desire to explain shooting a civilian while I'm on vacation. You wouldn't believe the paperwork involved."

That explained *everything,* he thought with a mental eye roll. He should feel incalculably lucky. He guessed she was military or CIA. She had all the right moves but not the look he associated with either so maybe not. "Glad I'm just a civilian to you." He adjusted his grip on the steering wheel. "Glad I'm just a P.I., too. I've never had to complete any paperwork when I shot someone."

"You really are a comedian, Stark."

And with that came more silence.

Just when they were getting to know each other.

He stole a glance at his new partner.

She'd leaned against the door and closed her eyes. Not that he could blame her. One of them should get some sleep.

He'd driven to Acapulco when he'd arrived in the country. The route wasn't that complicated. A navigator wouldn't be necessary until he reached the city.

Too bad this old heap didn't have a radio.

"You're not from the south or the west."

He smiled. "Couldn't sleep, huh?" She liked slipping in those little questions at the most unexpected moments in hopes of prompting an automatic answer.

"I'm from Southern California," she announced, shifting into a more upright position so that her head rested against the rear window of the cab.

"That doesn't narrow it down much." She fit the profile of a Southern California girl. Sleek, tanned body with long blond hair. And it explained the lack of any distinguishable accent and the total absence of manners.

"I grew up in L.A. You?"

"Florida."

She was staring at him again. "You don't get out much, do you?"

She also liked to keep a man humble. He, unlike her, had no tan. There wasn't a lot of beach time in Chicago. Work had kept him on overtime for the past year. "I don't live there now."

"I bet you don't like the cold climate of your new home."

Now she was fishing. Most any state, outside California and Hawaii, would have colder winters than Florida. "Not particularly."

"Married?"

"No."

"Engaged?"

"No." He sent her a surprised look. "You're interrogating me?"

"*If* I were interrogating you, Stark, a gun would be involved." She checked her phone. For the time, he imagined, since the service was sketchy at best. "Just wondering, that's all," she confessed.

"How about you?" Tit for tat, as they say.

"No and no."

"You're what…twenty-five?" Guessing a lady's age was dicey business but he felt confident he was on target.

"Twenty-nine next month."

He looked square at her. "Really?"

"Flattery will get you nowhere, Stark." She propped her feet, ankles crossed, on the dash.

He stared. With a couple of blinks to clear his head, he focused on the road once more.

"You?"

"Just hit thirty."

"How long have you been a private investigator?"

"Going on two years now."

"Before that?"

"Security analyst with the government." He stole a glance her way. "You haven't told me what you do." Sooner or later she was going to tell him to stop his harping.

He felt reasonably sure a full minute passed and she hadn't answered. She had the upper hand—and the only gun—and he knew she intended to keep both.

"If I tell you," she said after another long minute, "the dynamics of our partnership will be significantly altered. Is that what you want?"

Levi braked to a stop. He didn't bother pulling over to the side of the road. There was no traffic in either direction for as far as the eye could see.

More of those hushed seconds ticked off without her meeting his gaze and he wasn't saying what he had to say until she did.

He waited her out. She relented and turned her face to his. Finally he said, "It doesn't matter who you work for or where you come from. What matters is that we made a deal to find what we came for. Is that good with you?" This game had grown monotonous.

She nodded. "Yes."

He lifted his foot from the brake and hit the road once more.

Accomplishing this mission was the goal.

That was all either of them needed to know.

Chapter Eight

6:48 a.m.

Casey needed caffeine. Right now.

They were approximately forty minutes outside the city.

She might make it that long.

She glanced over at her partner. He'd crashed an hour ago. Casey had gotten an hour or so of sleep the first leg of the journey. She'd watched Stark fight the need for sleep until she'd threatened to drag out the Beretta if he didn't pull over. Men. They refused to admit any suggestion of weakness.

Finally he had surrendered and she'd taken the wheel. Not a minute too soon, apparently. The big tough P.I. had been dead to the world ten minutes later.

Now that it was nearly daylight Casey's

wicked side had been distracting her with the urge to study the man. Good thing there was no traffic. That vein of sheer feminine greed she'd failed to tame just wouldn't let her have any peace. Yes, the guy was pure eye candy. No denying that. He'd stretched out those long legs, snakeskin boots propped on the rusty old dash. The jeans he wore embraced his body with the same enthusiasm as an ambitious lover.

No man should look that good in blue jeans. And yet he definitely did.

The need to know more about him was eating her up. But getting answers required giving answers. Not an option. A frown creased her brow. Sometimes she felt... lonely. Okay, she'd allowed the word to fully form in her brain without her mother's prodding. Maybe that knock on the head had rattled more than she'd realized. Ached like the devil, that was for sure.

The day she'd graduated from UCLA she'd been hired on as an intern at the Agency. Having a father and an uncle who were high on the food chain had ensured her a spot. Three years later a transition into field operations hadn't gone over quite so well with her family. Casey hadn't let that stop her. Nothing had ever stopped her. Work was her life.

Relationships were repetitive and needy.

Her errant gaze once again drifted from the road to the man sleeping next to her. What fun was conforming one's life around the needs of another? Especially when no one could really be trusted. Not like that. She'd had her share of dates and mini-relationships and, just like the last one, they were more trouble than recreation. Uncle Thomas's single status said it all. Lucas had stayed single until he was fifty when he took the plunge for the first time and married Victoria. Why should Casey be any different?

Her mother warned that the closer she grew to thirty, the stronger the urge to procreate would become. Well, she hadn't said it exactly like that but the idea was the same. Casey had absolutely no compulsion to have children. Her work was too demanding. *She* was too demanding.

Kids. Husbands. No thanks.

Her mother was wrong.

Loneliness was a state of mind. Like

any other, it would show up from time to time and she simply had to show it who was boss. Relationships and all the required posturing weren't real. If a woman had to be someone else to keep her man happy, what kind of fulfillment was that? The need for physical contact, on the other hand, proved a little more relentless.

Levi Stark was not a good candidate for satisfying that feral instinct.

He roused. Speak of the devil. "Have a nice nap?" She braced for the warm, deep tones of his voice, then stretched her aching neck as if the battle was already lost. Her head must have been hanging like a limp doll's the entire hour she slept.

"We almost there?" Stark sat up and looked around.

Casey kept her attention on the road, but that little unruly streak that thrived in the DNA of her species wouldn't allow her not to sneak peeks from the corner of her eyes. "Almost." She tried to relax. "I could use some coffee, how about you?"

"Oh yeah. You want me to drive now?"

He was looking at her. She swallowed, tried not to inhale his scent. Funny thing was, she smelled like she needed a shower and he just smelled…good.

"I've got it." She mentally ticked off the names of all her cousins and their spouses and all the ups and downs those couples had suffered. Not a good way to discourage the random thoughts bombarding her head since somehow they always stayed together. Was Stark a good kisser? Skilled in bed? Frustrated, she moved on to the characters in her favorite novel. The idea that they all ended up happily ever after canceled that method for distracting herself as well. People were just weird and set in their ways. Why was it necessary to be one of a pair?

The forlorn glow of lights spotlighting a row of low buildings coming up on the right did the trick. The sign advertising gas prices loomed above the others, focusing her scattered thoughts on the need for fuel. For the truck and for them.

"We should get fuel." She slowed the truck and considered the storefronts in the hopes they opened early. A few scattered vehicles and welcoming interior lights gave her the answer she wanted. "Here we go."

She guided the truck into the parking lot and rolled up to the gas pumps.

"I'll get it." He opened his door.

Casey grabbed her bag and slid out of the truck. Her body ached from four hours on that hard, ragged seat. "I'll go inside and pay." And use the facilities. Assuming they had public restrooms.

Stark removed the cap from the gas tank. "Roger that."

Don't look at his eyes. Don't say anything else. Just go inside.

Casey straightened her skirt and smoothed her blouse. She looked like she'd had a rough night. Thankfully the skirt's dark color masked the dirt. The precariously hanging hem wasn't going to be camouflaged. Chill bumps tumbled across her skin right behind the caress of the crisp morning air. She hugged Stark's jacket closer around her and immediately regretted it. Wearing the jacket was like having him wrapped around her. The sun couldn't rise quickly enough to suit Casey.

As she neared the entrance to the gas station the distinct odor of meat frying made her stomach rumble. She craned her neck to verify that there was a small café next door.

Outstanding. She was beyond starving.

"Hola, señorita," the guy behind the counter called as she entered the gas station. He looked American, sounded that way, too. His butchering of the local language had the two locals loitering by the counter laughing at him. She wondered if he understood their unflattering remarks.

"Hola." She scanned the room. *"Bano publico?"*

The station attendant hitched a thumb toward the corridor behind him. "No paper in the toilets," he reminded her in perfect English. His two buddies sniggered and made crude remarks in Spanish as to what Casey was good for.

She smiled, realizing that she didn't have the energy to break their kneecaps, then walked purposefully past the counter and all three oglers. *Pigs.*

The bathroom wasn't as bad as she'd expected but that wasn't saying a lot. She did her business, remembered the warning about the paper though she couldn't see how anything this thin could stop up even twisted Mexican plumbing.

There was no soap but she scrubbed her hands and face anyway. The cool water felt good on her skin. Her hair was a tangled mess. It took some doing to smooth it out. She tucked the brush back into her bag and evaluated her reflection one final time. Not so bad considering. She smoothed her hand over the lightweight summer wool of Stark's jacket. The silk lining felt cool and yet somehow warm against her skin.

Casey shook her head at her reflection. Pathetic.

An extra tug was required to get the door open. Decades of paint and neglect had taken its toll. She jerked it open and came face-to-face with one of the deadbeats who'd been hanging around the counter.

"Need some help, *señorita?*"

The guy wasn't bad to look at. And he was dressed decently, clean. But obviously he had defective gray matter. "Not in this lifetime, *tonto*."

He dared to brace himself in the doorway. "A feisty one."

Casey smiled. "You have no idea." She

prepared to knee him in the family jewels but he suddenly moved. His body wrenched backward as if a cyclone had sucked him into its center.

Stark pinned him against the wall opposite her. "That's the ladies' room, mister. Maybe you should get your eyes checked."

The guy held his hands up surrender style. "No trouble, *señor*. My mistake."

Stark shoved him aside. "I don't think you want to make that mistake again."

Casey folded her arms over her chest and waited for Stark to face her. When he did she mentally squirmed from the intensity in his emerald eyes. "I had that under control, you know."

"Never said you didn't."

He disappeared into the men's room. Casey stared at the beat-up door for a moment. What kind of answer was that? Whatever.

Frustrated, confused, tired, hungry. There were numerous reasons for her irrational behavior. She explored the small store until she found the bottled water. All three of the men stationed around the counter stared at her but not one said a word.

It wasn't like Stark had kicked the guy's butt. Maybe it was something about the ferocity in his eyes that had been enough. Sheesh, she was going overboard about his eyes. There had to be something else far less hazardous she could obsess about.

Food. Her stomach rumbled again. They were here. They should eat.

The two interlopers backed off as she bellied up to the counter and paid for the gas and the two bottles of water. Stark showed up in time to open the door for her. How nice. Nice. Nice. Nice. He would be a much easier to ignore partner if he weren't so flipping nice.

"We should eat." The fragrant smells were stronger now. She was starving.

Stark considered the small café and shrugged. "Smells good. Why not?" He gestured to the screen door that served as an entrance to the establishment. "Grab a table and I'll move the truck."

Worked for Casey. She passed him the bottles of water. His fingers grazed hers in the transaction. She shook like she'd awakened to an earthquake. Hoped he didn't notice.

As he walked away she hugged her arms around herself. The still cool air whipped around her bare legs. Who wouldn't shiver? Without the sun it was downright cold. Just stop picking at it, Casey. She headed for the café. *Come on, sun,* she urged. She was not a fan of cold. How Lucas and Victoria tolerated Chicago weather she would never understand.

Speaking of Lucas, as soon as she had cell service or a hotel phone she needed to check in with him. Give him an update on what she had so far. But she'd need privacy from Stark to do that. Maybe she'd have Lucas check Stark out. Then she wouldn't have to worry about giving answers of her own.

The screen door whined as it opened, then slammed behind her. Two men had claimed one table. Across the room another accommodated a couple. Faded signs from similar joints on both sides of the border decorated the yellowed walls. The long row of windows that lined the front no longer sported curtains but the rod that had once held them remained, collecting dust. Most of the chairs presented had one leg too short, while the vacant tabletops lamented years of unkind treatment. The tile floor was uneven and in need of a serious scrubbing but the awesome smells emanating from the kitchen made up for all that and then some.

The waitress greeted Casey with a smile and told her to take the table of her choice. She selected the one closest to the back of the dining space and the employees-only kitchen entrance, then settled into a chair facing the front of the place. Better to have one's back to the wall and eyes to the front if one was to be prepared for an unexpected attack.

Stark walked in, only he didn't let the screen slam as she had. He surveyed the place, spotted her and headed that way, moving as soundlessly as smoke and every bit as smoothly.

Despite her best efforts, she watched him move, enjoying the show on far too many levels. She really had to figure this being-single thing out. It was as if dumping the cheating knucklehead she'd dated for a month had somehow tripped some sort of running-out-of-time sensor. Shaking her head to clear it, she picked up a menu and stared at the words, blurred by memorized images of Stark striding toward her.

He pulled out a chair and sat down. "Anything appealing on the menu?"

"*Huevos rancheros* sound good to you?" It was the first item on the menu and the only one she'd actually read at this point. No need for him to know this.

"Just about anything sounds good right now."

His gaze settled on hers and she quivered inside. Casey looked away. She was shaking only because she was starving, she told herself. She flagged down the waitress and ordered the food and coffee along with juice.

"We're only about half an hour from the city." He leaned back in his chair. "Hotel first?"

She faced him and wished she hadn't. They'd traveled all those hours in the dark with scarcely the ability to see anything. Now, as the sun climbed above the mountaintops, its warm rays reaching through the glass, she couldn't stop inventorying the details of his face. The day's beard growth looked appealing on him. The lack of sleep didn't even show. Instead of looking haggard, he looked rumpled and as sexy as—

The waitress plunked two mugs of coffee on the table, then two glasses of juice. She promised to be right back with their meals.

"Gracias." Stark gifted her with a smile that had the waitress floating back to the counter.

Casey had made a terrible mistake. She had miscalculated her ability to ignore her mother's recently amplified brainwashing efforts. Clearly that was the only answer to her current behavior. That and sleep deprivation and frustration. How many times was she going to inventory those excuses?

"Hotel first. Yes." She nodded enthusiastically. *Imbecile!*

The food arrived and saved her from herself. Casey dove into the eggs, refried beans and tomato-chili sauce with slices of avocado and guacamole. The juice was a heavenly blend of beets, carrots and cucumbers. But the best was the rich, dark coffee with just a touch of cinnamon. Just like the little Mexican place back home in L.A. made. Dinner there had been a Wednesday night ritual in the Manning household.

In no time she scarfed up the food and swallowed the last drop of coffee, closing her eyes to savor it. Anything, she could face anything now. Her eyes drifted open; her entire being felt rejuvenated. The sound of a sigh—her own unfortunately— snapped her to attention.

Stark was watching her. Staring at her, actually, a forkful of eggs halfway to his mouth. He blinked. "You really were hungry."

"That was splendid." The first descriptor that had popped to mind she refused to say out loud. Her mother would say it wasn't proper table conversation to include the word orgasmic. She needed to get her mother out of her head! "I can't believe they serve up such a tasty entree in a place that fits in so well with the scrub and tumbleweeds." More to the point, she couldn't believe she was unable to keep her head on straight around this guy.

Stark devoured the bite he'd had aimed at his mouth. "I'm not surprised," he said when his fork touched the plate once more. "The best diners I've discovered have been off the beaten path traveling between Tallahassee and—"

Casey leaned forward in anticipation but he caught himself. He'd almost said between Tallahassee and wherever he lived now. She'd nearly gotten that tidbit of information without having to reveal her own secrets.

But he wasn't so easily stumbled.

An awkward silence reigned for about two seconds. Thankfully, a woman entered with two kids hanging on to the skirt of her dress, both loudly vying for her attention.

Stark finished off his eggs and tortillas before downing the last of his coffee while Casey checked her cell to avoid eye contact or conversation. Her American carrier's service was still too sketchy to make a call. Sending a text, which might actually go through, was too risky. Classified meant no transmissions other than face-to-face or voice to voice.

"You got the gas," Stark said, "I'll get this."

That was one convenient aspect of

having a partner. She stood, pushed in her chair and headed for the exit.

At the door, she paused and surveyed the parking lot. Only one new vehicle, likely belonging to the newest hungry patrons. She pushed the screen door open enough to have a look at the entrance to the gas station next door.

Her radar still on full throttle, she walked the short distance to the truck. Stark, as usual, was right behind her. He inspected the back of the truck and the tires while she checked the cab. The old vehicle's door locks no longer worked so security was an issue.

Satisfied that no one had tampered with the truck, Casey slid into the passenger seat. She preferred to give directions at this point. She was lead in this mission. Oddly, it was she who needed to remember that. Reaching into her bag, she snagged the 9mm and nestled it against her thigh on the seat.

"You have a hotel in mind?" Stark asked as he got in behind the wheel and started the truck. "Or a certain section of town maybe?"

She hadn't done her research on the city since there had been no cell service and she hadn't known before interrogating Fernandez that Acapulco was her destination. "I don't know the area so I have no input other than something close to the club where Alayna works."

"You seem to have a good command of the language," Stark suggested, "so we can always ask for directions."

Casey had wondered about that. Seemed strange for a decent P.I. firm to send a man on assignment in a country where he didn't have a reasonably good grasp of the language. The bigger firms typically employed a staff with a wider array of assets, including various languages. She considered the man behind the wheel. Evidently his was a small, boutique firm. She resisted the concept that *low-rent* might be a more apt decision. Stark had class. Most low-rent P.I.s did not. She'd heard horror stories from her colleagues who had been forced to utilize P.I.s as assets from time to time.

"Works for me." This whole situation was bugging the heck out of her. She stared out the window as he pulled out onto the sandy road. It wasn't just this ridiculous physical attraction to Stark, it was working in the dark. Not having the relevant background info on him. Casey had worked a lot of missions. Each one came with its own surprises and risks. But she had never, ever worked so closely with a man about whom she knew so little. Even the dodgiest contacts came with a background profile.

This was probably a bad idea.

"Stark." She turned to him. "We need to talk."

The crack of a gunshot echoed a split second before metal dinged just over her head.

Casey grabbed her 9mm and ducked.

Stark swerved. "Looks like Fernandez did more than run."

"Just drive," Casey ordered.

Chapter Nine

Levi cut the wheel in a hard left. Casey swung toward him but managed to get off a shot at the Jeep in pursuit.

"Can't you go any faster?" she shouted over the roar of the strained engine.

A bullet glanced off the side mirror, cracking it.

"This is all she's got." The truck bounced with a cut to the right.

The Jeep rammed the back of the truck.

They launched forward. Casey banked off the dash.

"You okay?" He glanced at her but couldn't look long enough to evaluate her condition.

"For God's sake don't worry about me!" She scrambled back into position on her knees in the seat.

Miles of wide open terrain lay between them and their destination. At least another twenty or thirty minutes to Acapulco's outlying villages.

They were in trouble here.

As if to verify his assessment, the rear windshield shattered and a bullet lodged in the dash between him and Casey.

He shook his head and tried to shove the accelerator through the floor.

Casey was struggling with the passenger door.

"What're you doing?" he asked her.

The rush of air from the window she'd rolled down caused the truck to sway. She turned in the seat, facing him and stuck her right foot into his lap. "Listen carefully, partner."

If he hadn't been worried before, he damned sure was now. "What?" Another bullet thunked against the truck.

"Give it all she's got. When they're right on our bumper, swerve to the left and let off the gas immediately."

What the hell did she have in mind?

"Oh yeah." She took another shot at the

Jeep via the missing rear window. "And hold on to my ankle."

He sent her a doubtful look, his heart punching his sternum like a boxer in training.

"Go!" she shouted.

Pushing the truck for all it was worth, he wrapped his fingers around her ankle and held on tight. His attention split between the road and the rearview mirror.

"Here they come." He stopped breathing.

When he could no longer see the Jeep's front end in the rearview mirror he swerved left and let off the gas. The truck slowed as if he'd hit the brake. The Jeep rushed up next to them on Casey's side.

"Don't let go!" she yelled at him.

His fingers tightened on her ankle.

She thrust her upper body out the window, leveled her weapon and fired twice, three times.

The Jeep bumped the passenger side of the truck. The truck jostled wildly. Levi fought the steering wheel, barely keeping the truck on all four wheels.

When he dared glance in the rearview mirror again the Jeep was fishtailing out of control behind them. As he watched, it flipped onto its side and skidded to a stop.

Only then did he blow out the breath he'd been holding.

With the truck under control, he glanced at Casey. "You okay?"

She was on her knees again, watching behind them. Laughter burst from her throat. He checked the mirror to see what was so funny. The two *hombres* were attempting to upright the vehicle.

Casey collapsed in the seat. "Mercy, that was close."

"Too close." Levi swallowed back the panic that had swollen in his throat those last few seconds.

"You can turn me loose now." She wiggled her foot.

He'd forgotten. Another breath hissed past his lips as he forced his fingers to release.

She faced forward and twisted open a bottle of water, downing half of it before she took a breath.

Levi shook his head. This was wrong. Way wrong. He turned to stare at her.

"Don't slow down," she ordered before

he could speak. She made a breathy sound, kind of a chuckle. "Those guys are persistent. You have to give them that."

He stared forward, tried to calm down. Not possible. He wasn't going to pretend the past eighteen or twenty hours hadn't been off-the-charts bizarre. He had questions and by God she was going to answer them.

Anger lit in his gut.

He'd tried to get right with the idea that none of it mattered as long as they accomplished their mission but he had been wrong. He couldn't do this.

He gritted his teeth and let the fury simmer. He drove, fast, just like she said, until he reached the outskirts of the city. At the first row of businesses he encountered, he whipped into the parking area. The truck jostled and bounced.

Casey swore and grabbed her bag from where it had landed in the floorboard. "What the hell are you doing, Stark?"

He parked in front of the convenience store and shut off the engine. "The engine needs water." He didn't know if it did or not but that sounded like a reasonable explanation.

"We have water," she called after him but he was already out the door. He shoved it shut and kept walking. A smart man would cool off a bit before confronting a woman. Usually he was reasonably smart.

Somehow that had changed amid long silky blond hair and big blue eyes. Not to mention shapely legs and skimpy panties. Then there was the way she'd savored her breakfast. He'd almost lost it watching her lick that spoon. How could a woman that gorgeous be so damned crazy? She had to be out of her mind!

Levi didn't slow down until he was inside the convenience store. Halfway down the first aisle the crazy woman caught up with him, that big fringy bag resting on her hip. He ignored her and focused on trying to decipher the Spanish labels.

"What's wrong with you?" She frowned up at him. "The truck is fine. We need to get swallowed up in that city instead of hanging out here where we'll be spotted easier."

She was right. He knew this. He picked

up a bag of chips and attempted to determine if they were regular or barbecue. A cola would be nice, too. Didn't matter that he wasn't even hungry.

"Stark! What the hell are you doing?"

He looked up, as did the attendant at the counter and the five other patrons perusing the aisles.

"Look," she said more quietly. "Let's just calm down and talk about whatever's bugging you."

Calm down? Bugging him? Levi jammed the chips back on the shelf and grabbed her arm. He dragged her toward the far side of the store, right past the counter and behind the newspaper and magazine racks where no one was standing around staring at them. She didn't resist, in all probability because they'd both already drawn too much attention.

When they were out of direct view of the other customers he turned on her. "Who are you?" They had just survived a scene right out of a high-octane action movie, 3-D stunts included. He was just a P.I. But she...she was no P.I. At least not one like he'd ever met.

Her face blanked. Gone was the frustration, the irritation. There was absolutely nothing to read. She tugged her arm free of his hold. "We're wasting time. Do you want to do this or not?"

Another blast of outrage rammed into his gut. He moved his head side to side. Yes, this mission was of the utmost importance; and yes, they were wasting time. But he wasn't moving from this spot until he knew the truth.

"Who are you?" he repeated.

Her gaze narrowed. "You're scared." A smile lifted the corners of that lush mouth. "That chase back there scared the hell out of you."

A laugh rumbled up from the fury boiling in his gut. "That's good, lady. But not good enough. Who are you?"

"Just admit it, Stark," she insisted. "You were scared. That was new to you and you can't take it."

He fisted his fingers to prevent reaching out and shaking her. "Stop evading the question, Casey. Is that even your real name?"

She reached up, straightened his collar. "You know what your problem is, Stark?"

He shouldn't have looked at her…not directly into her eyes like that. Maybe even then he could have maintained control if…

If she hadn't stared with such longing at his mouth. If the world had stopped turning at just that second… If anything…something, had happened. He might not have lost complete control. But he did and so did she.

He kissed her or maybe she kissed him but it was game over either way. No more anger. No more frustration. There was just her soft, lush lips pressing against his. She tasted wild and sweet and just plain womanly. His arms went around her waist and he lifted her against him. Her fingers got lost in his hair.

He needed her closer…needed more. They collided blindly with a rack of magazines, sending the latest issues flapping to the floor like a flock of startled birds.

Lost in the taste and feel of her, from somewhere in the back of his mind he registered a tap on his shoulder that yanked him back to reality. Casey pushed out of his arms as he turned around. The lady from behind the counter started ranting at them in Spanish.

Levi blinked away the haze of utter insanity.

What the hell had he done?

Casey hurriedly grabbed up the magazines, apologizing in the local language as fluently as the lady glaring at them had spoken.

Levi helped pick up the rest of the magazines but didn't manage a decent breath until the clerk had stalked back to the counter.

"Let's go, Stark." Casey placed the last magazine in its place and executed an about-face. She went for the exit.

He couldn't move for a moment. Frustration, primarily due to his own actions, should have been the reason, but it wasn't. Truth was he couldn't resist the opportunity to watch her hips sway as she walked away.

He was in serious trouble here.

9:32 a.m.

LEVI MADE THE DECISION to leave the truck parked two blocks from the hotel in a service alley. He hadn't seen any sign of Fernandez's goons but that didn't spell relief. Trouble could show up anytime, anywhere.

The Hotel Americana sat right on the bay directly across the street from Club Delicia. The six-story hotel worked for their mutual purpose.

Though Levi hadn't seen the point in letting the presidential suite, Casey had insisted. He closed the room's elaborate double entry doors and dropped his bag on the floor. She'd already stashed her bag in the en suite in preparation for hitting the shower.

The room was massive with ornate detailing from the lavishly carpeted floors to the soaring coffered ceilings. The nightly rate equated to approximately half his weekly salary. Ridiculous.

Casey opened the French doors that led out onto the balcony. "What'd I tell you, Stark?"

Yeah, yeah. The exorbitant rate was worth paying since the room had two balconies. One overlooking the bay, but, more importantly, another facing the street and Club Delicia.

Levi joined her on the balcony. He had to admit the view was stunning. Unfortunately his eyes were not on the bustling city scene below but on the woman beside him. He shut them tight and castigated himself. He hadn't drunk the water or eaten anything that would make him loco but he definitely had gone down that path.

"Snap out of it, Stark." She whacked him on the shoulder. "We're alive and still on target. That's half the game."

"You want to shower first?" He needed some distance and a few minutes to get his head together.

She waved him off, apparently more interested in the vista. "You go ahead. I want a long, luxurious bath in that amazing tub. You won't want to wait me out, believe me."

Levi rounded up his bag and shut himself inside the enormous bathroom. He leaned against the door and worked at erasing the images of her soaking in that made-for-two marble tub that started reeling in his head the moment she mentioned her plan.

Food and caffeine hadn't gotten him back on track. Sleep deprivation had to be the problem. Not once since he'd begun fieldwork with the Colby Agency had he experienced such difficulty staying on track.

He'd been shot at before. He was trained for this. Why the hell couldn't he keep his feet under him?

Maybe a shower would clear his head. Incredibly, the separate shower, including full body sprayers and glass on three sides, was larger than the tub. Complimentary soaps and shampoos lined a built-in nook in the shower wall. He turned on the spray of water and set it to hot, chucked his boots and stripped off his clothes.

He stepped into the fancy, tiled mini room, let the water slide over his skin and grimaced. Too hot. He adjusted the temperature and then just stood beneath the broad-spectrum mist. The tension slowly melted from his aching muscles. He scrubbed a hand over his face, blew off the idea that he needed to shave. Later. This felt too good to move. He turned his back and let the rain of heat work its magic on those tense muscles. Oh yeah. This might take longer than Casey had anticipated. She might be sorry she'd given him first dibs.

He wasn't worried about her taking off on him. He had the name the same as she did. Finding and interviewing this Alayna was the next step. If they split up and started asking questions separately they could end up with the same result here as encountered in Pozos. They had to work together. For now.

The instant her image formed in his head his body reacted. A blunt craving rippled through every muscle as he replayed that crazy kiss…over and over. Arousal was instantaneous.

Cool air swept through the shower and he opened his eyes.

He was greeted by Casey's smile. "Sorry. I just need something from my bag." Her eyes drifted from his, traveling downward so slowly that his lower anatomy reacted as strongly as if she'd trailed her lips down that same path. When she'd finished her tour she smiled at him again and crossed to the counter where her bag was.

Levi grabbed a bottle of shampoo and dumped enough on his head to lather a gorilla. He didn't care if it dripped into his eyes. Maybe he could burn her image from his retinas.

After she'd cleared out, it took several minutes to rinse his hair. That really had been a stupid idea. A quick scrub of his body and he was ready to find a towel. He checked the room before exiting the shower to make sure she hadn't strolled back in.

Shaving crossed his mind again but he passed. Dressed and smelling like a perfume shop, he made his big exit. It had taken some time, but he had his head together now. He had her figured out. The kiss, the invading of his shower time had been about keeping him off balance. That, he decided, was her method of operation. None of it meant anything. It was all just a distraction ploy.

Well, he was onto her now.

Surprisingly he found her crashed on the couch.

Her blond hair glistened against the red and blue silk pillows. Completely relaxed by sleep, the feminine details she tried so valiantly to mask with toughness were breathtaking. Especially the lips. His mouth watered at the memory of her taste.

He shook his head. So much for having his head together. Yeah, he was really onto her now.

The French doors stood open. Theirs was an invitation he couldn't decline, particularly since standing around in here and gawking at her would be detrimental. He walked out onto the balcony and surveyed the street. This assignment had given every impression of being simple. More an exercise in intelligence gathering than anything. But the whole situation had taken a wildly unexpected turn.

Who else would be looking for the goods on this enigma who called himself Slade Keaton? The timing felt like far too much of a coincidence. One more to add to the growing mountain of evidence that Slade Keaton was not who or what he presented himself to be.

Levi glanced back at his new partner. Was she working for Keaton? If the past few hours were any indication, she was the perfect ploy to ensure Levi was unable to accomplish his mission. Apprehension mounted inside him, layering the doubts and piling on more questions. Though he couldn't deny she had been helpful. Getting out of that hole would have been impossible without her assistance. Then again, he wouldn't have been in that damned hole if not for her poking around in his assignment. Fernandez had warned Levi that someone else was in Pozos asking after Keaton and that she had arrived after Levi, making her presence keenly suspicious. Putting any faith in Fernandez's word, however, would be like leaping off this balcony and expecting a sudden gust of wind to break the fall.

In her defense, Casey had gotten Fernandez's men off their tail in an admittedly risky maneuver back there on that deserted stretch of road. One that had put her own life in jeopardy as well as Levi's. Then again, no one appeared to have been injured in the exchange of gunfire or the final showdown. Fernandez's men were, lucky for Levi and Casey, seriously bad shots.

Then again, had the whole scene been just one big production for Casey to gain

Levi's unconditional trust? Could she really be working with Keaton and Fernandez to throw Levi off track?

Where had she come from? Who did she work for? Why show up at the same time he did and allow her presence to be known? Someone as skilled as she was was surely capable of operating beneath the radar of her mark.

So many questions. No answers.

Levi turned to study the sleeping woman.

Who the hell was she? He'd asked that question over and over and he still didn't know.

More importantly, what power did she possess that had left him so totally…powerless?

Chapter Ten

Club Delicia, 9:45 p.m.

"We should split up."

Levi wasn't sure that was a good idea. His gaze swept over his partner yet again, no matter that he mentally kicked himself each time he made that monumental mistake. He resisted the urge to lick his lips. Casey Manning worked hard to show just how tough she was. She despised any indication of weakness. That had to be the reason her appearance tonight got to him this way. It was so opposite of the Casey he'd come to know these last twelve hours. Strange how so much could happen so fast.

The red dress hugged her body snugly, showcasing every delectable asset. Sky-high red stilettos added another mile to her shapely legs. He swallowed against the tightening sensation in his throat. She'd tucked up her hair in one of those sexy, loose styles that begged to be undone. His fingers itched to delve into that silky mass and hold her close as his lips got more intimately acquainted with hers.

"Stark." She elbowed him. "Did you hear me?"

He dragged himself back to reality, to the woman he didn't know and couldn't trust. "Sorry. Truth is, that dress keeps distracting me." No need to lie. She wasn't blind. "I'm not a big fan of red," he added just to make himself feel better, "but it looks... nice on you."

Casey smoothed a hand over the sleek fabric. "Good. That was the intent." She frowned. "Not to distract you, of course." She surveyed the crowd in the enormous room. "Them. The dress is for them."

Levi tugged at his collar and mumbled, "Lucky them." A trip to the hotel boutique had outfitted her with that IQ-lowering dress. She had insisted he wear a suit. Black jacket, black trousers and black shirt. Unlike her, he would fade into the background.

"We splitting up or what?" She searched the mob of faces. "Someone out there has to know Alayna personally. Friends, co-workers. I intend to find them."

"As long as we maintain a visual on each other." He would be able to spot her any-where in the crowd. Sure there were other women in the room wearing red, but not one who stood out the way Casey did. This step of the mission included having each other's back. The danger element had al-ready reared its ugly head twice over.

"You've got my number," she reminded him. "Let me know if you need me and I'll do the same."

The service was still a little spotty as far as calls went but sending or receiving texts was no problem. Casey melted into the throng. Levi felt torn between follow-ing her and doing his job. Every male in the club would want to know her. Women were abducted every day, particularly down here. Again, he was out of his mind. If he'd ever met a woman who could take care of herself, it was Casey.

Levi checked his cell phone to ensure service hadn't dropped completely. Later he would call Victoria. She was the reason he was here, not Casey Manning. He had to remember that.

Levi threaded through the fringes of the swarm, staying close to the bar that curved around the room for as far as he could see. The club's dome-shaped roof made for a soaring ceiling, and tremendous acoustical problems, he expected. Plush gold fabric lined the walls and ceiling in an effort to alleviate the issue. Mosaic tile covered the floor in a pattern of reds, golds and blues, at least the parts he could see. He wondered if tonight's occupancy had exceeded the fire code or if Acapulco even had one.

People dressed in every manner of attire flanked the bar and tables. A large, glittering stage ringed the center of the space. But the most troubling feature was the balcony that crowned the room, high above the stage. An equally thick crowd swayed to the music on that level, too. Anyone wanting to keep an eye on someone below would have the perfect vantage for it. Grand staircases, one to the west and one to the east, flowed upward, providing access to that area. Problem was getting through the crowd to reach the stairs and then weaving between the clutches of partiers hanging out on the steps. It was a strategic nightmare.

He marked Casey at the bar on the other side of the room. Men had gathered around her as if she were the star of the show and had generously offered autographs. Watching the attention they showered on her made his lips tighten. She laughed and tossed that luscious mane of hair. He shook his head. It was another blonde that he needed to be on the lookout for.

He and his partner—he glanced at her again—had toured the area around the club and hotel most of the afternoon, pretending to be just another pair of tourists here for the pearl-white beaches and explosive nightlife. She'd worn a more conservative pale blue dress today to fit the profile of doting girlfriend. Even then, sans the red dress, he'd had trouble staying focused. At that time, his distraction had fit with his cover. Too bad it hadn't been just an act.

Tonight was a different story. He was a single man on the hunt and he needed to step more fully into character. Like Casey.

Another look confirmed she was deep into character. Irritation sprouted deep in his gut.

Focus on the assignment, Stark.

They'd learned a few details about Alayna today. She lived nearby but no one could say just where. She owned Delicia, having become the owner only three years ago. Before that, as far back as ten years, most who knew her recalled that she had been employed at the club. None were aware of her last name, only her show which likely meant that Alayna was not her real name. Fernandez, it seemed, had gotten most of the details about her correct.

So far, if they'd had a tail, Levi hadn't spotted anyone. That would be good news if he were on his A game. Unfortunately, he wasn't nearly at his best. He may have missed more than he was prepared to admit.

He paused at the bar long enough to order a sparkling water with a twist of lime. Time to step up to the plate and do what he'd come here to do. Find the truth, or as much available information as possible, about Keaton. Whoever this Alayna was, these were the people who knew her best.

Applause drowned out the music. Levi faced the stage to see a gaudy swing lowering slowly from the ceiling. A woman dressed in a sequined costume, long shimmering legs crossed, waved to her adoring fans. Blond hair streamed like ribbons of silk down her shoulders.

So this was the infamous Alayna.

Her feet touched the stage floor and she hopped out of the swing. The crowd went wild as a host of other dancers rose on platforms from beneath the stage and took positions around the star. The music evolved into a sultry, evocative rhythm and the show began.

Levi scanned the faces where he'd last marked Casey's position, but he didn't see her. He swam through the river of bodies, moving around the club in a pattern that left no niche unexplored. Where the hell was she?

The performance on the stage continued while his personal drama played out below. Why would she disappear on him now? Their mark was finally in eyesight. Had Casey been waiting for just the right moment to ditch him? Worry and frustration fought for top billing. He'd known that trusting her was a risk. He'd hoped to get a better feel for whether or not be could rely on her but that hadn't happened. Instead, he'd spent all his time distracted by her beauty and her unpredictable actions. She had kept him guessing down to the wire.

And he'd danced just like a puppet on the end of that dangling wire. He'd waffled back and forth about trusting her. He had been a fool.

Levi knew one thing about Casey Manning for an absolute certainty. She was a master at distraction. Nothing she did could be trusted as real.

Too bad he'd come to that realization just a little too late.

Fernandez had been right about something else, Levi realized. Alayna was blonde, yes, and she was also beautiful. Like Casey. Was she a master of distraction as well? No one questioned knew her last name, he remembered. Some had lived in this area of the city their entire lives and they knew almost nothing about the woman's personal existence.

Levi set his drink on a passing waiter's tray. He turned all the way around, looking at but not really seeing the mass of faces. He only had eyes for one.

What did Keaton have to do with this place or this Alayna? The music suddenly sounded deafening. The notion that he'd been had, that this entire exercise had been a ruse, pounded in Levi's skull.

"There you are."

He turned to the woman who'd tugged on his sleeve. His partner. And just like that, he was back to square one.

Casey draped her arms around his neck. "Dance with me, Stark." Her smile dazzled him, drew him in like a beacon in the dark.

His arms went around her small waist; his hands settled on the curve of her bottom. He searched her eyes, her face, in hopes of finding some hint of the truth.

But she would never let him see beyond the charade she had plotted for him.

Casey tiptoed and pressed her cheek to his. His ability to breathe fled along with the last of his good sense. "I found her personal manager," she whispered into his ear. Her arms tightened around his neck. "I was told he's closer to her than her own mother."

"Mother? She has family here?" If Alayna was Keaton's sister, that would make the mother his as well. Casey's hair caressed Levi's lips, dividing his concentration. He refused to let the sensation distract him the way everything else about her did.

"This guy didn't know the mother." Casey twined the fingers of one hand into his hair. He tensed. "But he mentioned a mother repeatedly and insisted the personal manager is the key to getting close to Alayna."

"Is this personal manager interested in getting closer to you?" Levi winced at how the question sounded. Intensely possessive. Riddled with jealousy. The way her body was exchanging signals with his it was a flat-out miracle his brain still functioned at all.

She sighed, her breath whispering across his ear. He trembled. She was killing him. The song ended and relief attempted to invade his taut muscles, chasing away the rigidity.

But she didn't let go. She pulled him even closer and pressed those lush lips to his already oversensitized ear. "Afraid I'm not his type."

The hot, wild tension she'd wound so tightly released in one swift whoosh. He drew back, stared into those alluring blue eyes. "What exactly does that mean?"

She chewed at that full bottom lip, making him ache to savor that same spot. His mouth watered.

"He'll be far more interested in you."

The seductive fog of intense yearning cleared instantly. His first instinct was to accuse her of only reconnecting with him for that reason. Otherwise she would have gotten what she could from this manager guy and left Levi still muddling over his next move and wondering where the hell she was.

But they were here to get information. What did the reason or how it happened matter?

It didn't.

"Introduce me."

Casey took his hand. "This way."

They cut through the crowd, her soft fingers curled around his making him want to pull her back in his arms and just let their bodies take control. As insane as it was, he didn't care at the moment whether he could trust her, he just wanted to touch her. How had she cast such a spell on him in a mere twenty-four hours? The sensual music slithered from the speakers, snaking around his chest and squeezing out the air. The shadows created by the mood lighting were filled with couples seeking pleasure and no one cared because that was why they were here.

Casey's destination appeared to be an exclusive sitting area beyond the stage. A cloud of velvety colorful drapes hugged the white leather sofa and chairs, providing an element of privacy. As Casey approached, leading him like a disobedient puppy, the man seated in the center of the crowd raised a hand and those around him scattered like butterflies, flitting into the swelling crowd of partiers.

"Jazz, this is Stark." She tugged him

down to the sofa next to her. "Levi Stark. He's the movie producer I told you about."

Levi schooled his expression. Movie producer? He guessed he wasn't just the single guy looking for a good time anymore.

Jazz—what a name—offered his bejeweled hand. "Welcome to Delicia, Mr. Stark."

The music was softer here, allowing for conversation at a normal decibel. Levi shook the man's hand. "The pleasure is all mine, I'm certain." Jazz was a head shorter than Levi, a little pudgy around the middle and whatever hair hadn't been robbed by male pattern baldness he kept shaved. The saying that the clothes made the man was particularly true in this case. Though he was quite ordinary-looking, his attire glittered almost as radiantly as that of his employer.

"Don't kill me, Stark," Casey said, feigning repentance, "but I told Jazz that you came to Acapulco scouting for a location for your next movie."

She couldn't have prepped him for this encounter?

"Tell me about your movie," Jazz encouraged. "I'm so intrigued. Of course, you must know," he said to Casey, "we get every manner of celebrity here. Alayna has entertained them all, from rock legends to princes."

Levi exchanged a look with Casey who offered no help at all. "It's a musical," he announced in light of where they were and with whom he hoped to gain a meeting. If Casey had already suggested anything differently and didn't clue him in, Levi might just strangle her. A glance at her throat had his gaze sweeping down to investigate the enticing cleavage revealed by that damned red dress. With great effort, he swung his attention back to Alayna's personal manager. "I'm interested in a setting very much like this one."

"Do you have a star in mind already?"

This Jazz character spoke perfect English with positively no discernible accent. "Actually," Levi began, hoping this would take the conversation in the right direction, "I find Alayna quite striking. Her voice. Her dance skill and, unquestionably, her photogenicity." Was that even a word? As long as it sounded authentic.

"She's beautiful, isn't she?" Jazz practically purred.

"She is." Levi felt confident a real producer who considered beautiful women all day long for various projects wouldn't go overboard with the compliments. "Are you authorized to discuss her availability?"

Jazz smiled. "I am the only person authorized to discuss her, period."

Casey squealed and squirmed around like a high school cheerleader sidelined for the homecoming game. "I love this place." She placed a hand on Levi's leg, sending a stream of heat straight to his crotch. "You have to make this work, Stark, no matter the cost."

A definite glee lit in their host's eyes.

"Let's just see what we can do." He patted the hand that continued to linger on his leg. She did a little more of that giddy couch dancing. He'd never wanted to be leather more than he did right now.

"First, Jazz," Levi said as he reclined into the soft, thick sofa, "when can I meet her?"

Jazz blanked his face as he considered the question. Now he intended to play hard to get, it seemed. "She rarely takes meetings with strangers, Mr. Stark. I hope you're not offended."

"Understandable." Levi stood and thrust out his hand. "I appreciate your time. Mine, unfortunately, is limited. I'll be in the city for two more days."

One, two, three pulses of shell-shocked silence elapsed with nobody moving. Casey looked crestfallen but said nothing. The Jazz character had frozen like an ice sculpture at a celebrity wedding. As if desperation had abruptly cracked the ice, his face reflected the turnaround.

"Tonight." Jazz was on his feet in a flash. "Perhaps I can arrange a meeting after tonight's performance. I'm sure Alayna would be disappointed in me if I snubbed a man such as yourself on her behalf."

Levi let him sweat for a few seconds more. "Very well. You may give the details to my assistant."

He walked away.

Levi had his doubts about this guy. Either way, whether a peon with delusions of grandeur or the close associate he claimed, Levi figured the guy would go to any measures to make tonight happen. Everybody wanted to be a star.

Levi hadn't realized until he reached the bar that his heart was pounding.

This could actually work, putting this mission back on track in spite of his incompetence up to this point.

He ordered a beer and exhaled a ton of tension. Whatever else she did, he had to hand it to Casey. She'd conjured up a break. That was more than he had done. A whole lot more.

The bartender left a bottle of the house favorite and moved on. Levi drank, allowing the cool effervescent brew to slide down his throat, quenching his thirst for hydration but doing nothing for the other hunger that raged through him. He settled the half-empty bottle on the counter and released another of those big breaths. He had lost all shred of perspective. Nearly two years of experience and training had gone down the drain.

Casey appeared next to him. He saw her reflection in the mirror behind the rows of liquor bottles first. Or maybe he saw the red dress first. It was still calling to him. Making him sweat.

Her arms went around his neck and she popped up high enough to lay a big kiss on his jaw. "You did it!"

Was she kidding? She'd found the guy. She'd set up the meeting and guided the conversation. Levi had put in an appearance that may or may not have been convincing.

Scooting up onto the bar stool next to him, she waved at the waiter. "Tequila, *por favor*." She flashed the frenzied man one of those killer smiles and he instantly became her slave, ignoring the others pressed against the bar.

"Stark, why are you drinking beer?" Casey demanded, incensed. "We're in Mexico. You have to drink tequila. It's the law."

She snapped her fingers and added another shot of tequila to her order even as the barkeep approached with the first shot in hand. Unbelievable. Casey thanked the man, passed one shot to Levi, then lifted her glass. "To a successful partnership."

To say he was out of his mind would have

been the understatement of the millennium. This moment, right now, proved it. "Success." He raised the glass and downed the shot. The smooth, crisp fire warmed a path all the way to his belly. He seemed to recall watching this same scene play out between her and Fernandez back in Pozos.

Levi really was screwed here.

Casey huddled in close to him. "So, we have a meet with Alayna at one. Get this." She lifted her face to his and whispered in his ear. "We're having dinner in the restaurant next door."

Anticipation erased all the other frustrations of the past twenty-four hours, instantly sharpening his senses and kicking aside his misery. "The restaurant is open at that hour?"

Casey shook her head, excitement igniting fireworks in her blue eyes. "They stay open for her when she decides to entertain special guests after the show."

Reality intruded a fraction. "This Jazz guy took the bait that easily?"

"Finish your beer." She slid off the stool. "We have some time to kill."

That sounded like trouble. Not to mention she had evaded his question. Levi left cash on the bar for their drinks and turned to his partner. "How do you plan to kill this time we have?" He'd already decided not to call Victoria till tomorrow. He'd have more information then, assuming this meet went down.

"You'll see."

Once again Casey caught him by the hand and started through the crowd. He stalled. When she turned back to him, he shook his head then leaned close so she could hear over the music. "I don't like surprises."

"Trust me." She moistened those amazing lips. "You'll love this one."

That was exactly why he should say no. But he didn't.

Chapter Eleven

Casey needed Stark to go with her on this. If he balked... She'd just have to tackle that obstacle when the time came.

He wasn't going to like it. Didn't matter that she had only met him about twenty-four hours ago, she had his number and it was ten. Don't dive into anything without at least ten seconds' notice and/or ten logical reasons to make the jump.

She, on the other hand, was a one. Give her a second, or less, and/or one good reason and she was good to go.

The memory of that kiss back at the convenience store attempted to invade her senses again. She cut it off, bullied it back. A consequence of her handling methods. Nothing else. She had pushed his buttons until he'd reacted the way she wanted. As admittedly enjoyable as the kiss had been, it didn't count. None of this was real. It was the game and winning was all that mattered.

Casey intended to win. Losing—the equivalent of failure—was not acceptable.

Stark dragged her back to him a second time. "Where are we going?"

Time to turn up the persuasion in order to turn down his reservation. She specialized in persuasion. He was not immune. That part had already been substantiated. Immunity required immense self-discipline in the area of emotional engagement.

A slow turn put her face-to-face with her reluctant partner. She stretched up onto her toes, placed her hands on his broad shoulders, and leaned close and whispered in his ear, "Trust me, Stark. I haven't let you down so far." She allowed her lips to graze that erogenous zone.

This time when she tugged on his hand, he didn't resist. She continued slicing a path through the crowd. He followed. That was the thing about guys like Stark; about most good and decent people, for that matter. They wanted to believe. Wanted to trust in others. Particularly if they had no logical reason to distrust or disbelieve. Basic human nature.

Casey didn't trust until it was earned and maybe not even then. She definitely didn't believe anything she heard and little of what she saw. She'd learned that the hard way in this business. She'd learned a lot of things. Like the fact that people acted and spoke the way they wanted to be perceived, prompting the reaction they desired. She'd learned all that relationship stuff was merely superficial garbage.

That was exactly why she dated but didn't do real relationships. Just ask her last boyfriend. He'd called her an ice princess. All work and no play. So what if she was? Did that make her selfish—something he'd also called her? Relationships were for the weak. Casey Manning was not weak.

The expansive clubroom gave way to the chic lobby from which a narrow corridor led to the dressing rooms of the performers and ultimately to a dead end, an employees' entrance. Three other exits, two sides and one rear, provided emergency exit routes from the clubroom for patrons. The corridor was Casey's destination. The only obstacle that stood in her way was a key card reader.

A grin spread across her face. Except she'd already taken care of that obstacle. She had the needed key card. Lifting it from one of Jazz's groupies had been too easy. The star-struck fan would never miss it. At least not until the show was over. Judging by the number of cocktails the handsome young man had consumed he would likely believe he'd lost it.

Casey had under two hours.

Loads of time.

All she needed was a crowd to block the view of the door from the security camera that monitored the lobby. The building's security appeared adequate to put off the amateurs, but not nearly adequate enough for a professional. Casey headed for the main entrance.

"I need air," she called to Stark.

Outside, she selected a spot near the open doors and turned to her partner. She draped her arms around his neck and smiled widely for anyone watching.

His arms went around her as if the

act were as natural as breathing. "Is this the surprise?" Laughter from one of the clutches of passersby on the street briefly drew his attention.

"This is step one."

He searched her face, narrowed in on her gaze, looking for the deception he feared even as every part of him wanted to believe. Hard as she tried not to, she got lost for just a sec in those jewel-colored eyes of his. The man had some incredible eyes. Her emotions might be immune but she wasn't blind.

"I see." He gave a little nod and kept whatever other questions he had to himself. Her secrecy annoyed him. The need to play nice restrained anything more than a negligible outward display of that irritation.

A foreign sensation, doubt in her judgment, seeped deep in her chest. She ruthlessly staunched it. No one was that nice. So nice that she should feel remorse or guilt or whatever it was for keeping him in the dark. For all she knew, he could be plotting a strategy of his own.

Didn't matter as long as the mission was accomplished.

A thick crowd of clubbers climbed the steps leading to the lobby. "That's our cue." Casey threaded into the mob. Stark did the same.

Inside the lobby, she clasped his hand and went for the door blocking her path to the dressing rooms. One eye on the crowd, she swiped the key card, got a green light and pushed inside.

Casey didn't draw in a decent breath until the door was closed behind them. She scanned the corridor for cameras. None visible. It never ceased to amaze her that the general consensus regarding areas beyond a secure door was that they didn't require cameras. A mere lock, however state-of-the-art, rarely kept trouble out and security in.

"Dressing rooms?" Stark asked, his voice low.

"Hers is the one in the middle."

Casey sprinted that way. Stark trailed after her but didn't hurry. She had breached the room and was assessing the layout before he strolled in. The room smelled like flowers. She could still hear the music from the club as it reached a crescendo. Apropos.

She felt an upsurge in their investigation coming. Finally.

"Nice touch," Stark remarked, "lifting that key card."

"Yeah."

The room had no windows and only one door. She opened the door and took a look into a massive closet filled with costumes. A quick inspection of the walls behind the hanging wardrobe left Casey frustrated. "It has to be here."

Stark lounged in the open doorway. "I might be able to help if I had a clue what we were looking for. Photos? Papers?"

"Nothing like that." Damn. There had to be an exit here somewhere. She shifted her attention to Stark. He was right. He could help. Getting accustomed to the idea of a partner, however temporary and superficial, required an additional mental step on her part.

"Did the owner of the key card give you a rundown on the floor plan, too?"

Now she was insulted. "Give me a little credit, Stark. When he discovers the key card is missing, I wouldn't want him connecting the timing of the disappearance with a floor plan discussion with me. One of the waitresses told me about the dressing rooms. She brings drinks to the dressing rooms sometimes."

"So what're we looking for? Something in particular you're expecting to find?"

Still suspicious, was he? As for expectations, she couldn't say specifically. She was good but she wasn't that good. She didn't see through walls or leap tall buildings, though she had been known to leap off them when the need arose. At the moment, she had a hunch. "No one on the street we interviewed had any idea where she lives. They rarely see her outside the club. That means just one thing to me—"

"She either lives in the club or she has a route in and out that no one knows about." Understanding lit in his remarkable eyes. "Very good, Casey."

Stark had a point about the photos and papers though. She added those to her search as well, though she doubted the woman was that careless. Cautiously placing each item back exactly as it had been, the two of them explored the room thoroughly.

The room was full of costumes, makeup and hair products. Nothing else. Not even a stash of cookies or chips. Framed photos of Alayna with various visiting celebrities and newspaper and magazine clippings lined the wall. Casey studied the face of the woman who was reportedly the sister of Slade Keaton. Brown eyes went along with the blond hair. High, prominent cheekbones. Sculpted lips. She was beautiful. She had little in common as far as appearance went with her supposed brother.

Stark stood in front of the enormous floor-to-ceiling mirror studying his reflection. Casey moved in beside him. "The suit looks good on you." The statement was a calculated maneuver, yet it was the truth. Appreciating his physical assets made her more human than she cared to feel, but it didn't make her susceptible to his charm. A very important distinction.

A frown scrawled across his handsome face as he leaned a little nearer the mirror. "This is it."

She'd checked out the mirror already. It had no hinges, no levers. "You think?" Had she missed something? Doubtful but possible.

As if he'd read her mind, they both started to run their fingers over the edges of the ornate frame. Stark tugged. It didn't budge.

But… "Do that again." When he gave her a questioning look, she said, "Try to move it again."

He curled his fingers around the frame and tugged. In the mirror their images shimmered the tiniest bit, then stilled.

Casey reached out and touched the reflective glass. It didn't move. She pressed a little harder…and it moved. Oh yeah. Adrenaline wired her senses. This was it.

As the glass swung inward, she stepped over the frame onto a rock floor. A similar rock wall faced her. She reached out and touched it. Solid. Cold. She moved closer and discovered that it wasn't just a hiding place or dead end. Anticipation screamed through her veins. This had to be how Alayna moved to and from the club. A narrow opening to the left led into a passageway. It was dark as pitch and tight, if the opening was any indication. "There's a passageway here. I can't see where it goes. Too dark."

Stark joined her in the cramped space. He reached beneath his jacket and withdrew his weapon. "I'll go first this time. I'll check it out and see if I can find a light before we stumble into trouble."

Fine by Casey. "Too bad neither of us smokes." They needed a light.

The passageway was black. Like the hole they'd fallen into last night. The light from the dressing room valiantly attempted to turn the corner into the passageway but fell short.

"Let's have a look." Stark moved past her and through the narrow opening. Over his shoulder he said, "Wait until I assess the lighting situation before following me." There was a brief hesitation and then, "Check the mirror for smudges where we opened it. Make sure it's closed."

She didn't bother letting him know that she'd already planned to do that. In case he'd forgotten, she had twice as much experience at this as he did. Grabbing a tissue from the dressing table, she cleaned the smudge from her fingertips off the glass.

Once she'd closed it, leaving her in absolute darkness, she waited, the seconds ticking off like bombs in her head while Stark traced the rock wall with his fingers as if it were Braille.

A faint glow peeked around the corner. Instinctively, she leaned toward it.

"And there we go," Stark announced.

More of that anticipation ignited inside her as she joined Stark around that corner.

The passage was narrow and only extended a few feet before spiraling downward in an even narrower staircase. "If this is how she moves back and forth from her home, it gives new meaning to the term harrowing work commute."

Stark smiled and she had difficulty dragging in the next breath. He had a powerful smile and really nice teeth, too. The guy could do toothpaste commercials and sell lots of the product.

"Stay close," he suggested, taking the first step down. "There's no light switch. The lights are apparently motion sensitive. But if it goes black again, better to be close."

She followed close for fourteen steps.

Then they hit another long, narrow corridor. She couldn't hear the music anymore. Instead she detected more of a roar befitting the cavelike, musty-smelling setting. The occasional small dome-style light kept the darkness chased away enough to watch one's step.

Two more minutes of moving forward and nothing changed. It would be really nice if she could get her bearings. Were they moving east? West? Casey couldn't say.

Something solid stopped her. Stark. Before she could complain she got distracted by him trailing his fingertips over the rock wall. "What're you doing?"

"It's wet here. Really wet."

She peered at the wall, stepped close enough to touch it. He was right. Dripping wet almost.

"The water." His gaze settled on hers. "This is taking us to the beach."

That was it. "The hotel."

Stark nodded. "Maybe so."

They moved faster, an unspoken but mutual sense of urgency propelling them both. Any details they could discover might be useful. Keaton hadn't remained anonymous without the aid of those who knew and cared about him.

The sound of crashing waves and the smell of salty air greeted them as they reached the end of the narrow passage. But the exit wasn't straightforward by any means. A mini maze of twists and turns, each more narrow than the last, provided escape to the silky white sand.

Moving prudently just in case there was a security patrol in the vicinity of the secret passage, they headed for the stretch of beach directly behind the hotel.

"Wait." Casey stopped and removed her shoes. Stilettos and sand didn't mix. When she straightened Stark was staring at her the same way he had when she'd first dressed for the evening. "You really like the dress, huh?" She smirked, couldn't help herself.

"I'm reasonably certain all who've seen you tonight have liked that dress."

"In that case," she said as she plodded toward the hotel, "I chose wisely."

"You're thinking that perhaps Alayna is a permanent resident of the hotel."

Apparently he'd moved on from the subject of her dress in a hurry. "Perhaps," she replied. It seemed a reasonable deduction. "Could just be a private access to the beach." Who wouldn't enjoy a private path to a scene so tranquil? The sea air smelled salty and sweet at the same time, but it was cold just now. She shivered. Something else that reminded her of home. The warm days and cool nights, the contrasting aromas of nature's most powerful resource and man's irreverent ambition to pillage. Another little quake trembled through her. She missed home sometimes. A visit would be in order soon.

Warm silk settled on her shoulders and hugged her body. Her breath caught more from the scent of Stark suddenly cloaking her in his jacket than his chivalrous move.

"I thought you might be cold."

"Thanks." She blocked the unwelcome sensation of inner warmth that awakened deep inside her. This was a mission. He was her sort-of partner—more a pawn in her strategy. She wasn't supposed to be impressed by him or his actions. Guilt pinged her.

Just stop, Casey. You don't know this

man. He's the competition, not a friend or...whatever.

"Isn't our suite on the top floor?"

Casey snapped to attention, glad to put the disturbing thoughts aside. "There are two presidential suites on the sixth floor." Then she saw what had made him question the floor plan of their hotel.

It wasn't quite a full balcony like the one extending the living space of their suite or the one alongside it. The small half-moon shaped protrusion above their balcony appeared more like an architectural feature. Yet, there was a window or door. Something she couldn't quite make out that could very well provide access to another floor. A floor that didn't exist in the hotel's brochures or have a button in the public elevators.

"There has to be a private elevator."

"If there's a room up there, that would be my guess," he agreed. "Even if we're right, that doesn't mean the room is hers."

"We can't be sure of anything." They were speculating. That was half the game when gathering intelligence. If you didn't know, you fleshed out possible scenarios until you hit the right one.

"Could be for VIPs."

"Could be."

"Depending on how the meet goes," he offered, "it's certainly a lead we might want to follow."

"Certainly." Casey checked the time on her cell. "We should head back."

The walk across the white sand beneath the moonlight was quiet and strangely calming. The party crowd apparently preferred the dazzling lights and music along the streets to the soothing roar of the sea and the quiet glow of the moon and stars on the sand. Or maybe those who preferred the latter were making their own kind of quiet music in the shadows. The thought made her yearn for that kind of sweet escape.

Casey rarely experienced calm during a mission. And the only kind of escapes she generally took were from the bad guys. This sudden yearning was categorically out of character for her. She stole a glimpse at Stark. She banished the idea that he made her feel this way. The yearning had nothing to do with him. It was the place, she supposed. And the relief of being back in the field, even if while on vacation, after months of being in a cramped, artificially lit office.

"You have sisters and brothers back in L.A.?" The deep resonance of his voice washed over her, layering more of the serene insulation somehow generated by this place and this night.

"No. I'm an only." It annoyed the heck out of Casey that the word *lonely* echoed in her skull. She wasn't lonely, she was busy. She had no time for complications.

"Me, too." He chuckled. "My mother reminds me regularly that I'm all she has."

"No father?" Casey resisted the impulse to bite her tongue. She didn't want to encourage his questioning.

"He died six years ago."

His father's death still made him feel sad. She knew because the pain echoed in his words. She would not ask anything else about his family. No. No. No. Except… "Your mother never remarried?" Good grief! What was she doing?

"She swears she never will." He released a big breath that drew her attention straight to his mouth. "I wish she would. I'd feel better. But she says when you love someone like that, there's no such thing as an encore."

Wow. His mom sounded like Lucas. "You think she's lonely?" Seriously, she wasn't saying anything else. Not another word.

"How could she not be?" Stark looked at her as if she should be smart enough to know without asking. "She's fifty-five. Her companion of twenty-seven years is gone. That's gotta be tough."

Don't say anything, she told herself.

They were almost to the street. The noise would preclude the need for conversation then. Prepping for the meet should be her focus.

"You ever been married or engaged?"

Where was he going with that question? "No." *You?* banged at her skull. She would not ask! They'd had a similar conversation already.

"Me either." He slid his hands into his pockets. "Too busy, I think."

Forty yards to safety. She had to keep

slogging toward the street and the insulating noise of the crowd.

"Most of my cousins are married. House and kids to boot." He laughed softly. "My mother calls whenever someone announces their engagement. I can actually hear the wistfulness in her voice when she tells me."

Dear God. They had the same mom. Like hers, his mom should butt out. Casey knew from experience that wasn't going to happen. She'd been telling her mom to do exactly that for years.

"She's convinced I changed careers to avoid commitment."

"Did you?" Casey's eyes widened. She didn't just ask that! If asking the question wasn't perverse enough, she stared at him in anticipation of his answer.

"I was bored." He glanced at her, caught her staring, making her even angrier with herself. "I needed to be more involved with people. To help ensure the right thing happened more often."

Like not dropping a stranger into a bottomless pit and saving himself. Or insisting she wear his jacket when his thin shirt wasn't much more protection than her dress. "Bored is the excuse adrenaline junkies use for running into burning buildings and going into hostage situations." She felt him looking at her so she met his gaze. "Making sure the right thing happens is just another way of saying you like to win. Am I right?"

He stopped. Held her gaze for long enough to make her wish she had kept her mouth shut. "Is that your model for doing what you do, Casey? Like the risk you took back there on that deserted stretch of road? Or all the little things—like that dress— that you do to keep me off balance? Winning is all that matters to you, isn't it?" He shook his head. "If that's true, I feel sorry for you."

Casey was almost twenty-nine, and only once in her entire life had anyone ever said anything to her that actually got to her. Until tonight. Irritation immediately replaced the other foolishness. "If you don't win, what's the point?"

Walk away.

She put one foot in front of the other. When people got all emotional that was the best way to handle it. Just walk away.

Nothing that got said would be right or would really change the other person's stand on the matter.

Motorized traffic had obviously been diverted since the street between the hotel and the club was filled with pedestrians as if they had decided to bring the celebration to the streets and no one minded. It was well past midnight and the party was still wild and loud inside the club. When they stepped in, she could see Alayna and her dancers swaying and grinding on the stage in an erotic performance that had couples unabashedly devouring each other on the dance floor.

Cloying, perfumed sweat comingled with the essence of liquor, creating a sensual fragrance that ignited the senses. The perfect combination of visual and auditory ambience bound the carnal spell so completely that Casey wondered how it could possibly be broken without inspiring a riot.

Alayna had created a masterpiece of enthralling entertainment. Casey watched her lean body move to the notes. Every move, every step was choreographed in mesmerizing rhythm. She would be a challenging mark.

Casey would need Stark to distract her… if she was distractible.

HE DIDN'T LIKE CASEY very much right now. Her responses were contradictory to his protected view of people and life. She had to do something to alleviate that disillusionment or risk losing his cooperation.

At the bar he ordered a sparkling water and turned to Casey to see if she wanted a drink. She swept his jacket from her shoulders, dropped it on the counter and moved in close to him. "Dance with me, Stark."

He didn't immediately say no but he stared at her as if he were contemplating going in that direction.

She took his hand in hers and pulled him close. "We need to look like a couple if we're going to pull this off. You wouldn't be a movie producer if you weren't taking advantage of your young, naive assistant."

Reluctance in his movements, he allowed her to guide him deep into the throng of couples lost to their own stimulating interludes. Before she could put her arms around him, he pulled her close, pressed her intimately to his body and started to move.

The rush of heat and a frightening burst of desire stole her breath, made her tremble. As if he sensed that weakness, he held her tighter, leaned in closer until she couldn't breathe without inhaling the scent of him. Her cheek brushed the roughness of his unshaven jaw, spawning a desperate ache between her thighs.

Casey closed her eyes and fought the dizzying sensations. A few more minutes and they would be in position to start the next phase of this mission. She could deal with these unexpected feelings Stark evoked for a few minutes more.

It didn't matter anyway.

This wasn't real.

He couldn't be real.

Chapter Twelve

Andrew and Michael's was an Italian restaurant. The rustic décor didn't quite suit the elegant menu but Levi wasn't complaining. Amazing smells emanated from the rear kitchen. More importantly Jazz had announced that Alayna would arrive at any moment.

The door to the private dining room was flanked by members of Alayna's security team, two inside, two out. Jazz sat at one end of the long dining table. Levi and Casey had taken seats opposite each other near the end reserved for Alayna. Four male companions, more security, Levi suspected, had joined them at the table. The men had lots of muscle and familiar bulges beneath their jackets. Weapons, obviously. Levi and Casey's guns had been taken at the door, as had their cell phones. Levi didn't know about Casey, but he'd initiated the lock on his. If anyone attempted to break the pass code to his phone, the stored information would be deleted. The phone Levi could do without; the weapon was another story. He didn't like that naked feeling. Particularly when surrounded by an armed detail.

Jazz was enthralled with Casey. He directed the occasional question at Levi, but for the most part Levi's partner carried the conversation. Levi used the time to assess their surroundings and the security. That the two of them seemed to anticipate so easily their proper parts in this partnership continued to surprise him.

In all probability, that was something he shouldn't get used to. If nothing else, he had learned how unpredictable she could be. He'd learned something else as well. Casey Manning had been wronged. Badly. She trusted no one and believed in nothing but the work.

That truth bothered him far more than

it should. He wanted her to believe and to trust…in him.

Jazz withdrew his cell from his pocket and checked the screen. "Ah." He smiled widely. "She is here."

Following the reactions of the others around the table to this announcement, Levi rose from his chair.

Jazz hurried to pull out the reserved chair at the head of the table. The belle of the ball waltzed into the room, her steps as graceful as her moves on stage.

"Alayna, may I introduce Levi Stark and his assistant, Casey Manning." Jazz gestured to each in turn.

"Mr. Stark." Her voice was rich, almost deep.

Levi nodded an acknowledgmcnt since she did not offer her hand. Alayna spared Casey a brief, measured glance but said nothing. Casey smiled humbly, ever in character.

When Alayna had taken her seat, the rest settlcd once more. Three waiters rushed into the room, carefully placing salad plates arranged with fresh greens and topped with brightly colored accompaniments. Then the three stepped back and waited to serve the needs of their hostess.

Alayna's attention came to rest on Levi. "Your presence tonight surprises me, Mr. Stark."

"How so?" He would put the ball back in her court. If she led he was far less likely to make a misstep.

"I usually receive notice when a man of your professional status schedules a visit to my club."

He didn't doubt it a bit after the photos he'd seen in her dressing room. "I doubt you were any more surprised than I. This visit was not on my agenda."

Alayna's gaze narrowed as if she were endeavoring to discern if she had just been insulted. Silence congealed in the room. Casey telegraphed him a sharp warning with her eyes. He, too, had a part to play and bubbling with enthusiasm was not in the profile. This was her gig. She should appreciate the intricacies of his part.

When he had stretched Alayna's patience far enough, he said, "My assistant insisted I catch your show while scouting locations." He acknowledged his partner with a subtle dip of his head. "I rarely scout for talent these days. It usually comes to me." He mentally ticked off the trauma-filled seconds that followed, allowing the silence to swell once more.

"Since you're here," Alayna said finally, "I presume you enjoyed the show."

"I did." He forced the instinctive tension in his muscles to unwind. He had to take it slow, not appear too eager.

"Then you are interested in my show?"

"I'm intrigued by *you.*"

Alayna relaxed in her chair for the first time since arriving. "As I am intrigued by *you.*"

"Perhaps we should speak privately."

No one had touched their food or drink during the stilted exchange. Levi predicted that everyone at the table was less than pleased by his suggestion. Everyone except Casey. She would be livid. All the more reason not to make eye contact with her.

Alayna turned to Jazz and he immediately stood. Without a word he left the room, the others filing out after him, including Casey. She shot Levi a withering look on her way out. She would have to trust him the way she expected him to trust her.

Now that the room was cleared, Levi rested his full attention on the lady who Fernandez had claimed was the sister of Slade Keaton.

"You have questions." Her expression provided no clue as to what she might be thinking.

"I do."

"Perhaps I have answers." One corner of her mouth tilted upward just the slightest bit, fracturing the ice that seemed to encase her.

"Assuming we were to reach an agreement," Levi broached, "can you be available to devote the time required to the project?" What sorts of ties did she have, if any? There had been some mention of a mother. He needed to learn as much as possible without deviating from his profile. Now that they were alone, it was the time to push harder.

"Perhaps."

Nice hedge. "You don't have commitments that would divide your attention?" He clasped his hands in front of him. "I find it very frustrating when family obligations get in the way."

"You have no family, Mr. Stark?"

The way she watched him, prepared to pounce on the slightest deviation from character, would have been a bit unnerving except that he'd spent the past twenty-four hours with Casey Manning. He had full confidence that he possessed nerves of steel.

"Let's just say I have no obligations that pose a threat to the needs of my work." He could hedge with the best of them.

"I can see how that would be fortunate for a man in your position."

She had either taken the bait without reservation or she was playing him to buy time for her own agenda. "Why don't we put our dance cards away, Alayna?" He matched her poker face. "There are many personal questions you'll need to answer. I don't like surprises and those who bankroll my projects don't either. Is Alayna a stage name?"

A smile widened the tiny fissure in her perfectly composed features. "Yes. But my name is irrelevant. My family obligations are as well. My commitment at Delicia is at my leisure. Does that answer your question?"

"I see."

"So there is no misunderstanding, I have no previous film experience. I have only what you saw tonight to offer. Either it is what you're looking for or it is not. The money is irrelevant."

That gave him a whole lot of nothing. "No criminal record?"

"Of course not."

"You're American?" He was nearly certain she was. Either that or she had at least one Anglo parent.

"By birthright I am, but this country is my home."

She was warming to him, one degree at a time. "Although much of the project would be filmed here," he explained, trying another avenue to ask the same questions, "we'll be spending a great deal of time in the States. Is that a problem?"

"I never leave this country."

Why, he wondered. "That will be an issue."

"In my experience," she countered, "we do what we must to obtain what we want."

Touché. Now was the time to take it up another notch. Throw her a curveball. "Sadly, I must answer to my investors. One of them in particular insists that part of every project be filmed in his beloved city of Chicago. Perhaps you've heard of him. Slade Keaton?" Levi leaned forward and blatantly studied her. "I'm certain he would be very disappointed if I failed to communicate that requirement. I'm also certain he will be very interested in you."

Her eyes glazed with cold fury. "Who are you?"

"You do know him." No question there.

She stood, her chair rocking precariously behind her. "We have nothing further to discuss."

Levi blocked her path when she would have moved toward the door. He couldn't let her get away just yet. "I have questions about Keaton." She started around him and he placed his hand on her arm, prompting an icy stare that warned her tolerance threshold had been reached. "The matter is urgent. I was told that you're his sister. If that's true, you may be able to help."

"You have made a mistake, Mr. Stark."

"I don't think so. I think you do know him and I'm not going to stop until I find the answers I need." He was pushing it here and she still hadn't called in her security. Some part of her was curious.

She inclined her head and studied him. "You have no idea who you're dealing with, do you?"

Not exactly the reaction he'd hoped for. "Right now I'm dealing with you."

"No, Mr. Stark. You have far greater problems than me." She searched his eyes. "I regret to inform you that as of this moment you are living on borrowed time, as they say."

"Is that a threat, Alayna?"

She squared her shoulders, signaling that she was done here. "It is merely a statement of fact, Mr. Stark. Now, if you will step out of my way, there will be no need to involve security."

Not just yet. "Who is Keaton?"

For five thundering beats of his heart he was certain she wouldn't answer, then she said, "He is a man trained to kill anyone who gets in the way of what he seeks. If it is you he seeks, he will find you no matter how long it takes and then he will lie in wait until the perfect moment to act. You will not escape."

"How do you know this?" Was she his sister or a former lover? Levi needed answers. "Who are you?"

"That is irrelevant. I will give you one final advisement, Mr. Stark. Please hear me well. You and your friend should run. Now. Your actions have awakened a sleeping dragon and you will be devoured by her."

Alayna walked around him. He didn't try to stop her.

Levi stood alone in the room, the walls suddenly closing in around him. His instincts screamed at him. He had to call Victoria. He had to warn her.

"What the hell happened?" Casey stormed his position. "What did you do, Stark?"

"We have to get out of here." He glanced around, felt the urgency building for reasons he couldn't fully understand. They had to move quickly.

"Tell me what went down in here, Stark."

He grabbed her hand. "As soon as we're out of here."

She started to argue but he shut her up with a look.

Levi wasn't sure if she fully got it but whether she did or not, she didn't resist.

To his amazement their cell phones and weapons had been left at the front entrance with the restaurant's security guard. And both weapons were still loaded. Who was this woman? Levi shoved his weapon into his waistband. Casey's went into her bag. As much as he'd prefer they keep them palmed, they couldn't go out into the street like that. Not even in Mexico.

He held tightly to Casey's hand as he weaved through the clutches of partiers on the sidewalk. Going back to the room was not a good idea. They needed some place safe to lay low until he figured this out and touched base with Victoria.

The absolute certainty of Alayna's warning, more so than her words, had him worried. She could have called in her security at any point during the exchange. He and Casey had been unarmed. But Alayna had not done that. She wasn't worried about what he or Casey might do to her. No, her concern lay elsewhere. With Keaton? Maybe. That was the part he needed to know.

Alayna suggested someone else would be coming. She was so certain, she'd even left their weapons. That was the part that worried Levi the most.

Casey yanked hard on his hand and he kept moving. They needed more distance from Delicia and whoever Alayna feared might be watching. A dozen yards later, Casey balked, dragging him to a stop. He had no choice but to turn around.

"Not here," he warned. He knew she had questions, but there were too many people here. Too much noise. He needed to make a call and get a safe house address for regrouping.

Victoria had warned that his safety was to come before all else. But he wasn't worried about himself at the moment. It was his boss and this unpredictable blonde he wanted to protect. He wasn't sure how Casey would react to this turn of events.

"We need to get off the street," he told her.

The urgency he felt must have finally penetrated. "Okay. I get it. We need dark and quiet."

With her in the lead, they covered two blocks in record time. She navigated him into a cantina that looked less than reputable. The place was jam-packed but somehow she effortlessly threaded through the bodies and found a table in the darkest corner of the joint. Too bad it was occupied.

Casey reached into her bag and pulled out a wad of cash and thrust it at the couple. *"La mesa, por favor."*

The man looked to the woman who smiled and reached for the cash. They grabbed their drinks and cleared out.

Casey sat down before he could pull out a chair for her. He collapsed into the remaining one.

"How bad did you blow it, Stark?" she demanded.

He sincerely appreciated her confidence

in him but this was not the time to challenge her trust issues. As soon as he gave her the dirty details he had to call Victoria. Didn't matter what time it was. That unrelenting sense of doom kept hammering at him.

"According to Alayna, Keaton is dangerous," he explained to Casey. "We need to contact our clients and see how they want us to proceed. He has to be stopped." Somehow. Having gotten that out, he caught his first real breath as he scrubbed a hand over his mouth. This was way wrong. Every atom in his being vibrated with urgency.

"That's all you got? That he's dangerous? Damn it, Stark."

"Did you hear me? This is—" A bump against his shoulder startled Levi. He shot to his feet, his hand instinctively going for his weapon.

Two women giggled and apologized profusely in Spanish. He picked out the word *banos* and realized their table was next to the restrooms. He blew out a chest-full of tension. Turning his chair around to put his back to the wall, he sat down again and reached down deep for calm. But he couldn't find it.

"You don't get it," he growled at Casey who still glared at him.

"I get that she was our only lead and you blew it." She shook her head. "I should never have left you alone with her."

The exchange between him and Alayna kept playing over and over in his head. What had he missed? "There was something she said besides the fact that he was dangerous." The warning had been pretty straightforward and still it nagged at him. He missed something.

"Did she admit to being his sister? Did you at least get that from her?"

Her. He almost had it. "She said we should run. Now. That we had awakened a sleeping dragon." What else? There was more. "That we...would be devoured by *her.*"

"She said dragon?"

Levi nodded in answer to her question but his attention was centered on the rest of what Alayna had said. *Her*...not him.

Would she have spoken about herself in

that manner? Maybe. He couldn't say for certain.

Unless, the *her* was Alayna's mother. Who else would be watching Alayna closely enough to be aware of her visitors or anything else going on in her life? A spouse? A lover? That she'd indicated a female didn't rule out either. But since a mother had been mentioned, he leaned in that direction.

Levi's gaze collided with Casey's. "I think she meant the mother, hers and Keaton's." It was a leap but the only logical one based on the intelligence they had so far. Levi scanned the crowd of revelers. Staying still like this was a mistake. They needed to move.

"We have to go." He reached for her hand as he stood. To his relief she didn't debate the issue.

The place had to have a rear exit. Going back out onto the street wasn't a good idea.

Evidently thinking along the same lines, Casey pulled him close and said, "This way."

Going right past the end of the bar didn't sit well with the bartender. His shout followed them into the kitchen. Casey didn't slow down. A dishwasher ranted at them in Spanish as they hustled out the rear entrance.

"I assume going back to the hotel is out." She didn't slow down as she spoke, dodging trash cans and the clutches of those doing their business in the dark of the alley.

"For now."

Casey abruptly pushed him into the wall of the nearest building and pressed her body against his. "You're certain she said *her* and *dragon*."

"That's what she said." Despite present circumstances his body reacted to the soft curves of hers. "Does that ring a bell for you?"

A group of men sauntered past, sniggering and making remarks about Casey's red dress. When they had passed, Casey resumed their trek along the alley.

"Not really. She may have been referring to herself," she suggested over her shoulder. "She's damned bizarre."

"Possibly." Bizarre was an apt description for the lady.

Casey stopped and Levi barely avoided

bumping into her. She faced him. "We need to know where she lives. If there's a mother, they may share a home."

She was right. But he needed to make that call. Had Casey already contacted her client about the initial meet?

Didn't matter. Alayna knew Keaton. They had no choice but to follow that lead, whatever the danger.

Though Victoria had reminded him that his safety was to be primary, the bottom line for him was her safety. And Casey's. Alayna had said Keaton would lie in wait until the perfect time. He had been watching the Colby Agency very closely for months now. That part was very disturbing.

Victoria was in danger.

Levi had an obligation to get to the truth. Whatever it took.

"I still say they could be living on the floor above our room at the hotel. If it exists," Casey qualified.

That risky avenue was their only real option at the moment.

Their only lead.

"We can't go in through the lobby." And

the hotel restaurant would be closed, ruling out that option.

"The side and rear exits are fire escapes and we'd set off the alarm," she added.

They were missing a step....

"If she uses that tunnel for movement from the club," he said, "we can tail her from there." He'd bet his life she had a private access from the club to the restaurant where they had met tonight. Alayna was a local celebrity, but her supersecretiveness was a little much.

Casey hitched her thumb toward the darkest part of the alley. "Down the street and then cross to the other side."

"Watch our backs." Levi palmed his weapon and took the lead. If his partner had a problem covering the rear she kept it to herself for a change.

He'd wondered if this partnership would work out when the chips were down. It seemed to work so far.

The possibility that Casey Manning was the *her* Alayna had spoken of and now intended to lead him into a trap loitered around the fringes of his thoughts.

This whole performance could be about

uncovering the name of his client. Casey could be the enemy.

Maybe he was a fool but he refused to believe that theory. She had come through repeatedly.

She was his partner until her actions showed otherwise.

THE BEACH WAS STILL QUIET. There had to be a popular beach hangout somewhere but, thankfully, not here. He and Casey had taken a position near the opening of the hidden passage. Not close enough to hear trouble coming but near enough to see any movement.

Casey dropped her red stilettos in the sand and fished her weapon from her bag. They each had a few bullets in their clips. Not enough to wage a war but enough to get by. Levi surveyed the beach and the water beyond. A couple of vessels had dropped anchor in the bay. Night-vision goggles would have been nice.

Beside him, Casey was restless. He'd insisted she take his jacket against the chilly night air. They'd gone over a route for slipping away if the need arose. He'd likely have to drag Casey kicking and screaming if she wasn't ready to go but he was prepared to do whatever it took to keep her alive.

"Why haven't you gotten married?"

Talk about coming out of left field. At her question, he turned to his partner though he couldn't see her face in the shadows of their surveillance position. "If I tell you," he challenged, "you have to answer the same question for me."

She pulled in a big breath, maybe for courage. "Fair enough."

He'd expected her to decline. Now he had to answer. A deal was a deal. "I came close once but she didn't want children." He chuckled, the sound self-deprecating. "We'd dated for two years. How could I not have known that?"

"Kids are a big commitment."

"Your turn," he reminded her. She wasn't going to change the subject.

The pause drew out long enough that he wasn't sure she intended to honor her part of the bargain.

Then, finally, she spoke. "We were co-workers—early in my career. He was older and this big hero. Charming, good-looking. I fell for all of it."

"Was he married?" Levi had a feeling.

"Oh, yes."

Man, that sucked. "That had to hurt."

"Hurt like hell for a while. But I got over it."

She stared at the ocean. Levi wished he could read her mind. He wondered if she kept everyone at arm's length like this because of that one jerk. "I apologize for the male species. I don't know how a guy does something like that and sleeps at night."

She laughed softly. "I asked him that very question. He said I needed to grow up and get with the program. Nothing is real but the mission."

Levi let the silence sit between them for a time. He doubted she would want to hear his advice but he'd never been able to hold back when someone was in pain. However long ago this bad relationship happened, it still carried a major influence in her life.

"That was his way of denying the guilt." Levi wished he could kick the crap out of the guy. Then again, Casey probably already had. "If what you do in life isn't real, there are no consequences. You're free to use and abuse anyone."

Casey kicked at the sand. "I think maybe he was right." She folded her arms over her chest. "I've watched too many so-called happy couples start hating each other and end up in divorce. None of it's real."

"That works, I suppose," he offered. "If you like taking the easy way out. You can't fall if you don't take the leap."

She had nothing more to say. He'd obviously said too much.

The timing worked out though.

A pale light filtered from the opening of the passageway tucked amid the jagged foothills of the cliffs overlooking the sea.

"Heads up," he murmured.

Someone was coming.

Chapter Thirteen

Chicago, 3:15 a.m.

Slade Keaton sat in the darkness of the brownstone that housed his office. His pulse thrummed loudly in his ears. He needed that call to come.

As much as he did not want his suspicions confirmed, he needed to know. Now.

Maggie was angry at him for avoiding her today. He should never have allowed her to get so close. But her coffee shop had presented the optimal vantage point for his surveillance needs.

A perfect view of the Colby Agency offices.

And he had been weak.

He'd made a foolish mistake.

One he already regretted.

He rubbed his jaw. The situation was

no longer within his control. He had taken every step possible to maintain that dominion, and still he had lost.

For two years he had waited and watched. The timing had required some tweaking but he'd made it happen.

Two years wasted.

His goal would never see fruition if what he suspected was true. Lucas and Victoria's trip to Mexico last month had changed everything.

Slade could only hope that the worst had not happened. The call he awaited would confirm his concerns one way or the other.

His next move would depend entirely on it.

Metal vibrated against wood as the screen of his cell lit with an incoming call.

"Keaton." The air stalled in his lungs.

"Contact was made."

Slade closed his eyes. He shook his head slowly from side to side. "Status?"

"You're not going to like it."

He didn't like any of this. "Just give me the status."

"The dragon has roused."

Resignation crushed down on his shoulders. "It's done, then."

"Affirmative."

Slade surveyed the dark room. Light was not required. He had memorized every crack in the wall. This life was over. Like the others before it, the name Slade Keaton was now useless.

"What do you want me to do?" the caller asked.

There were, however, loose ends requiring immediate attention.

"Whatever it takes."

"Copy. Whatever it takes."

"Call when it's done."

Slade ended the call and sat in silent mourning for a time. For the energy he had invested…the level of comfort he had achieved. Perhaps for the woman who owned the coffee shop as well.

Lucas Camp had no idea what he had started.

There would be war.

Chapter Fourteen

Acapulco

Casey braced to move.

She monitored their progress as Alayna, followed closely by Jazz and flanked by four of her security team, moved across the sand toward the hotel. A light blazed to life above the balcony of Casey and Stark's room.

Giving him a nudge with her elbow, she pointed to the floor above theirs. The floor that didn't exist. Their hunch had been correct.

Raised voices drew her attention back to Alayna and her entourage. Three new arrivals outfitted in black, including ski masks, surrounded the group. Casey's heart slugged through a couple of beats. Where the hell had they come from?

One of Alayna's bodyguards went for his weapon. He dropped in the sand. Another joined him. The hissing pops of the masked men's weapons had scarcely been audible over the crash of the waves.

Twenty yards was all that separated Casey and Stark from the encounter. They could overtake the gunmen....

As if he'd read her mind, Stark clasped her arm and held on tight. "Not yet," he murmured.

Unable to look away, Casey watched as the remaining two members of Alayna's security detail were executed. Her fingers itched on the trigger of her 9mm. They had to do something.

One of the men leveled his weapon at Jazz's head. Before he, too, could be executed Alayna raised a hand, apparently in his defense. A fierce exchange between her and the masked man who appeared to be in charge played out while the other two members of his party scanned the beach.

At last the man lowered his weapon. Alayna and Jazz were ushered toward the water.

The boats. Casey's attention swung to

the large vessels anchored offshore. The attackers had to have come from the water and one of those vessels. "If she gets aboard one of those boats we might never locate her again."

"Stay put," Stark ordered, "and cover me."

No way. Casey reached for him but he was too fast.

Stark moved across the sand, the moon spotlighting him as if he were on stage.

Casey couldn't breathe. She leveled her weapon and prepared to fire. If one of the gunmen turned around and spotted Stark she would put him down.

Stark was almost on the group. Casey eased from the protection of the rocks, her attention fixed on the movements in front of her. She rushed forward, her bare feet sinking into the sand, slowing her down.

"That's far enough," Stark ordered.

Two of the men whipped around. Casey dropped one, Stark eliminated the other.

The third, the one in charge, kept Alayna and Jazz moving toward the water. Casey sprinted after them. Stark reached the group first.

"Drop your weapon," Stark ordered.

Alayna stopped, got a nudge with the muzzle of the boss's weapon for her trouble. Jazz whimpered in fear.

The man, his weapon in Alayna's back, didn't speak, didn't lower his weapon and didn't turn around. Fearless, was he?

"Drop it or I will shoot," Stark repeated.

The blood roared in Casey's ears. What was wrong with this guy? Was he deaf? Or just stupid?

Cold steel nudged the back of her head. "You drop *your* weapon, honey," a male voice ordered in flawless English.

Casey braced to hit the sand and roll as another masked man rushed past her. She screamed, "Behind you, Stark!"

Too late. The gunman rammed his weapon into Stark's back.

Casey's weapon was snatched from her hand. She cursed herself for allowing a moment's distraction. The gunman ripped the bag from her shoulder and shoved her forward. "Move," he ordered.

As Casey stepped forward, the man in charge turned around and slugged Stark. He swung back, catching the guy with an uppercut. Casey smiled. *Good for you, Stark.*

A small outboard motorboat swayed in the water a few yards from the shore. Alayna and Jazz were forced aboard first. The lead man climbed in next. The cold water sloshed around Casey's legs as she and Stark were ushered closer.

Brutal arms wrapped around Casey's waist and hauled her into the boat. When the goon released her she elbowed him hard in the chest, aiming for the sternum. He yanked her by the hair and growled a threat into her ear.

She gave him a look that dared him to try putting any part of himself on or near her for the good it did in the dark.

Stark climbed in next to her.

The compact anchor was lifted from the water and tossed in the boat. The engine revved to life.

"You," the man in charge said to Stark, "you're the pilot."

The boat rocked slightly as Stark got into position to navigate. Alayna remained mute. Jazz fidgeted next to her. Two of the masked men were left behind as the boat cut through the water, headed, apparently, for the larger of the two anchored vessels. Yachts. One, some eighty or more feet in length. Large enough to serve as a floating home. A decidedly handy means of transportation when staying under the world's radar.

The spray of salt water filled the air, prompting a blast of adrenaline through her veins. The answers she needed likely waited on that vessel. Surviving long enough to pass along those answers was considerably less likely.

She hadn't said anything to Stark yet because what she suspected was highly classified. Many times during her career she had heard rumors about the Dragon. She'd even heard that the person designated as the Dragon was female. Elusive and deadly. There were few real details, more legends and fables than anything.

Casey turned back to the shore. The two men who had been left behind had cleanup detail, she figured. Four men had been killed on that beach. The scout who'd come up behind her could have easily taken out both her and Stark. There had been several opportunities before they were forced into the boat.

She and Stark had been spared for a reason.

Interrogation, she suspected.

There was only one thing either of them knew that would be of interest. The identity of who had sent them.

Casey rested her gaze on the yacht they were approaching. Whoever waited aboard the fancy boat should just bring it on because she would die first.

Truth was, if this was the Dragon they were dealing with, they were dead already.

Sunrise

CASEY HADN'T SEEN Stark in hours. Once onboard the yacht, they had been separated. She hugged his jacket around her and paced the luxurious stateroom. If a girl was going to be a prisoner, this was the place to be.

She'd heard no screaming. No gunshots. Nothing. She studied the sleek paneling on the walls, then the lush ceilings and carpeting. Soundproofed. Guests could be eaten alive in one stateroom and their neighbor would never know it.

The small windows were blocked by automatic darkening shades, preventing her from seeing out. But the time according to the wall clock was past seven-thirty. The sun would be up, heating things up.

More pacing. She had been doing that since the goon who'd manhandled her had stuck her in here. There was an en suite washroom. She'd taken advantage of that, washed the seawater off her skin, finger-combed her hair. Mostly to pass the time.

She rubbed her palms up and down her arms, relishing the soft fabric of Stark's jacket. His scent still lingered on the fabric—on her. She'd been wearing his jacket so long, her skin had drunk in the smell of him.

Would they kill him? Whoever *they* were. The *she* Fernandez had been referring to, obviously. Code name the Dragon, possibly.

Immensely dangerous, definitely.

Casey didn't dare give in to the need to sleep. Determined to find a way to escape, she had searched the room for any sort of usable weapon or hiding place. What she would give for a tire iron just now. She'd

found nothing. No eating utensils acciden-
tally left behind. No tweezers, scissors, nail
files. Not one thing to work with.

Lucas would be doing some pacing himself by now. She hadn't checked in as she'd
planned last night. Lucas would likely have
called her uncle. Maybe Uncle Thomas
would order a special ops team to retrieve
her.

And Stark.

If he was still alive.

She wanted him to be alive.

He'd been a good partner, as partners
went.

At the sound of metal against metal, her
gaze veered to the door. The lever lowered
and the door opened. Her nasty buddy, automatic rifle in hand, strode into the room.

"Sit," he ordered.

Casey rolled her eyes and plopped into the
white plush chair next to the sofa. The man
was Hispanic but with no lingering accent.
A grizzly beard and too-long, tousled hair
coupled with his black attire and S.W.A.T.-
issue boots labeled him a mercenary.

He stood next to her, the business end of
the weapon stuck in her face.

"Where's my partner?" she demanded. Not that she expected an answer but that was beside the point.

He kept his eyes on the closed door and his mouth shut.

"Where are we?" she asked, just to annoy him.

Silence.

"What time is breakfast?" She hadn't eaten in about twenty-four hours.

No answer.

"Were you born this charming or did you go to school for that?"

Casey crossed her legs and tapped her foot against the air. She was sick of waiting.

A moment later the door opened and a woman entered.

Casey started to make a wisecrack but words failed her as her brain assimilated what her eyes saw.

Female. Fiftyish. Short, spiky hair. Coal-black save for the invasion of gray streaks. Dark eyes set off by the deftly applied makeup. Tall, svelte. The charcoal slacks and sweater were tasteful and elegant.

Casey couldn't breathe for a moment. This was…impossible.

"I have just one question." The woman moved a few steps closer.

"I was about to say the same thing," Casey interjected, more to disguise her surprise than to show off her wit. "Are you Alayna's mother?" She looked more closely at the woman. The coloring was different but the eyes were the same. "I'm aware that Alayna is Keaton's sister. Does that make you his mother, too?" She put her fingers to her lips. "Sorry, that was two questions."

The woman smiled. "Clever, aren't you?"

"On occasion."

"I know who sent you."

Casey's sass fizzled. This woman couldn't know. Casey had to restrain her need to stare openmouthed at the woman. She looked exactly like—

"Why did he send you?"

"Let me see my partner," Casey bartered, "and I'll tell you."

Fury blazed in the woman's dark eyes that were eerily familiar. "Why were you sent here?" she repeated.

"Not until I see Stark." If this woman had already asked him that question and gotten the answer, she wouldn't need to ask Casey. Though they had been sent by different clients, the reason was the same.

Obviously she hadn't gotten the answer from Stark.

"I will have the answer," the woman promised.

"Didn't you ask your daughter?"

Her eyes went from burning up with fury to ice-cold. But if that was all she wanted to know, Alayna could tell her that. Was Alayna not talking to mommy dearest?

"Thirty years," the woman said, her lips tight. "Why has Lucas waited thirty years?"

Casey held her outward reaction in check. How did this woman know Lucas? Who the heck was she? Casey was not going to like the answer, she feared. "I have no idea what you're talking about. Who's Lucas?"

"Your godfather. Close friend to your uncle Thomas. I know both men far better than you ever will." The ghost of a smile haunted the mouth that obviously hadn't formed the expression in so long a miracle would be in order to bring about the real thing.

"I have no idea who you're talking about."

"Your name is Casey Manning. You're twenty-eight. You graduated from UCLA and went directly into the service of the Central Intelligence Agency. Your last performance evaluation cited you as reckless. That's why you were taken out of field operations and put on probation. Shall I ask my question again?"

"Since you know all the answers," Casey argued, "why go to all the trouble to bring me here? I left a perfectly good pair of stilettos on the beach back there."

The woman turned to her underling. "Take her below with the other one. Kill them both." With that the lady exited the room with the same flourish with which she'd entered. Casey was still reeling from what she'd seen.

How was this possible?

Somehow she had to get word to Lucas.

This was beyond bizarre.

"Get up." Dirty Man poked her shoulder with the rifle barrel.

Gladly. If she'd read between the lines accurately, he was taking her to Stark. Couldn't kill a man who was already dead, which meant he was alive.

Though she hadn't figured a way out of this yet, maybe he had. Or perhaps she would on the way.

There wasn't much to see but a richly paneled corridor between the stateroom where she'd been held and the narrow winding stairs that led down to the lowest deck. This deck wasn't quite so luxuriously appointed as the others. The deck hands and security detail likely populated this area. She supposed Alayna and Jazz were in one of the staterooms close to the one Casey had been kept in.

So far no avenue of escape had jumped out at Casey. She considered attempting to overtake the guy ushering her along but she needed to let this thing play out. On the off chance she escaped, she might as well leave with more information than she came with. And she needed to find Stark.

"Stop there," her guard ordered. "Stand to the side."

Her heart rate sped up in anticipation of seeing Stark.

The door was unlocked and shoved open and there he was.

A little beat up but still alive.

Casey entered the new cell with no coaxing. The urge to hug Stark made her chest flutter wildly. Instead she gave him a quick look up and down and nodded her approval. "I was worried they might have killed you."

His gaze roved over her body. The hunger in his eyes chased away the chill she'd been fighting for hours. "Same here," he said wearily.

His voice wrapped around her like velvet, made her feel safe. It was nuts. She wanted to tell him about the woman who had questioned her, but she couldn't. It was unbelievable. Impossible. She ached to talk about it.

But if she told him about the woman who had questioned her, she would have to explain about her connection to Lucas.

And Casey couldn't do that.

How was this possible?

The resemblance was uncanny.

The Dragon looked exactly like Victoria Colby-Camp.

Chapter Fifteen

Casey was alive.

Levi's knees weakened a little at seeing her. He wanted to hug her but she was searching their cramped quarters in hopes of discovering a way out. He'd done that already, twice.

There was no way out.

He didn't want to die but he accepted that fate as a possibility any time he was in the field. Far more than he wanted to survive, he wanted Casey to survive. Watching her search the room, his jacket practically swallowing her, filled him with regret that he hadn't been able to protect her.

His biggest regret, however, was the idea that he wouldn't be able to warn Victoria.

He still couldn't believe it. The woman who'd overseen his interrogation looked so much like Victoria she could be her sister, if not her twin. He'd been seriously rattled but he hadn't answered her questions. Even after some serious encouragement from her head security man—the one who'd brought them here. Levi gently swiped his busted lip with his shirtsleeve. Bastard.

Had the same woman interrogated Casey? She hadn't been roughed up as far as he could see. He was glad for that. She also wasn't saying much.

"Did *she* question you?" he ventured. He couldn't share the one stunning revelation with her. The chances of their walking away from this were minimal at best, but he couldn't break the promise he'd made to Victoria.

Who was this woman who called herself the Dragon? What connection did she have to Victoria? To Lucas? To Keaton? Levi's mind reeled.

Casey dropped her arms to her sides, obviously giving up on her search. "Yeah." She faced him. "It was weird. She kept asking me why I was sent here. She claimed to know who sent me." Casey hugged herself as if she suddenly felt cold. "She knew everything about me."

Could the situation get any more bizarre? The woman had listed off an entire background profile on Levi too. "She knew all about me as well. But what she really seemed the most interested in was why I came here." He shook his head. "The strangest part is that Alayna knows why we came. Why didn't she ask her?"

"Yeah." Casey walked past him. "I said as much. Didn't make her too happy with that comment."

That just didn't make sense. Then again, nothing about this mission had.

As Casey examined the door that stood between them and escape he noticed that the hem of her little red dress was only an inch or so longer than his black jacket. A smile tugged at his lips. He really, really liked that damned dress.

"I'm glad you picked that dress." The words were out of his mouth before he could stop them. Didn't matter. It was the truth. They were way beyond those kinds of pretenses at this point.

Her lips quirked. "I'm glad you're glad, Stark."

She stood there looking at him for a long time. A long, honest look. No arguing. No competing. Just looking. This couldn't be the end. Not yet.

Casey walked straight up to him, toe-to-toe. His heart thumped a couple of times.

"We have to get out of here, Stark." That vulnerability he'd thought he'd heard just once in her voice was back. This time it reached her eyes. "We can't die here... now."

Determination detonated inside him. "You read my mind." He brushed a strand of hair back from her cheek. "We're partners. We can make it happen."

Before he could contemplate kissing her, the door opened.

Levi moved in front of Casey.

"Let's go." The same man who'd brought Casey here gestured to the door with the rifle in his hands. "Both of you."

Levi held his ground. "Where are we going?"

"Let's just get this over with, Stark." Casey stepped around him and strutted toward the door, giving the guy a show he wouldn't soon forget. The guy made a cheap, sleazy comment but didn't lower his guard. He kept a close eye on Levi.

As Casey reached the door a misstep sent her sprawling across the threshold.

Levi braced.

The red thong did the trick. The slimeball took his eyes off Levi and that was all the opportunity he needed.

Levi rammed the guy's head into the wall. Casey rolled, grabbing the rifle barrel as she went and twisting it free of his grip. Another slam of his head into the metal casing around the door put him down. Levi dragged the guy to the far end of the room.

"Secure him," Casey said, keeping watch at the door.

"Roger." Levi ripped off the guy's shirt and belt and quickly hog-tied him. He removed a boot and peeled off a sock for a gag. He checked his pockets for a cell phone or a knife. No such luck.

He joined Casey at the door. "We're clear to move."

Being the unpredictable woman she was, she thrust the rifle at him. "Follow me."

"Whatever you say." He blocked images of that red thong from his mind. His throat felt parched. The woman had one hell of a great backside. He'd have to ask her about her stumble later, when they were relaxing over a margarita some place quiet and calming.

She moved quickly toward the narrow winding staircase that led upward. At the foot of the stairs he touched her shoulder.

"I'll take it from here."

She stepped aside, allowing him to pass.

Taking care that each tread was soundless, he ascended the stairs. He paused at the top, scanning the corridor and listening for any sound. Deserted. Not a peep. He moved fully into the corridor and waited for Casey.

Casey padded quietly past him. She stopped at the first door to the right and listened. She gestured for him to take a position on the other side of that closed door. Slowly, she reached out and pressed the door lever.

The stateroom was empty.

They moved from room to room and found the same. No clothes. No food or drink. Not the slightest indication that anyone had ever been there.

Their gazes collided. "They couldn't have vanished that quickly," Casey said. Like him, she couldn't believe her eyes.

"Only one way to find out." Levi started toward the next set of winding stairs, this one wider and more elegant than the last. He climbed quickly this time, still taking care to move as stealthily as possible. The crew, or other members of the Dragon's entourage, could be on the main deck.

But silence greeted him there too.

The sun beat down on his face. The salty air filled his lungs.

Where the hell was everyone?

"Stark." Casey tugged on his sleeve.

He followed her gaze, saw the pair of booted feet, toes up, protruding past a small dining table and chairs.

A knot formed in his gut as they approached the table. Casey checked the man's pulse and shook her head. He'd been shot, center chest, his weapon still in his hand.

Casey picked up his weapon, removed the silencer, then checked the clip. The fact that, other than the breeze, the waves and an occasional winged creature, they hadn't heard a sound since reaching this deck was flat-out eerie. If a housekeeping detail had been ordered, the weapons would have been outfitted with silencers to avoid unwanted attention. But why do this?

They searched the main and upper decks. Six crew members, judging by their uniforms, two security guards, and Jazz were dead. Each shot either center chest or in the back of the head. Only the crew members had ID. Evidently the identities of the others were part of the Dragon's many secrets. More silenced weapons had been left behind, but no cell phones or radios.

Levi surveyed the water. They were well out of the bay but he could still see the city of Acapulco in the distance.

Who the hell was this woman that she could leave such devastation and simply vanish? Obviously she had taken Alayna with her since her body wasn't among the others.

But how had they disappeared so quickly?

The other vessel. He surveyed the water. There had been two yachts waiting back in the harbor— this one and a considerably smaller one. It was gone.

"We need to talk to the guy downstairs." Levi turned to Casey. "He's the only one left." If he would talk, he had to know something useful.

"Then," Casey said, her voice grim, "we have to get out of here. If the authorities show up, we'll never see daylight again."

Unfortunately, she was right.

No need to use stealth this time. He and Casey rushed back down to the lower deck. Their captor-turned-hostage was attempting to wiggle loose.

Casey tugged the sock out of his mouth. He shouted a few choice profanities. "Save it," Casey warned.

Levi stuck the rifle barrel in his face. "Where did *she* go?"

The guy laughed. "Like she would tell me." He shook his head. "Her security got nervous about someone or something in the water. She ordered everyone killed, and left with her daughter. My orders were to kill you two and go home. I was the lucky one."

"Home?" Still crouched next to him, Casey dragged the muzzle of her weapon down his torso, allowing it to linger at his pelvis. "Where's home?"

Sweat had beaded on his brow. "Acapulco."

"You work for Alayna?" Levi asked. He didn't remember this guy as part of the security detail.

He wagged his head. "I work for her *madre*. I keep an eye on Alayna. Let her *madre* know when trouble shows up."

"Like us," Casey suggested.

"Fernandez warned me weeks ago that trouble was coming." He swallowed with visible effort. "I did my job."

Now they knew the connection between Fernandez and this so-called Dragon. At least they'd tied up that loose end.

"What do you mean they got nervous?" Levi had a hard time believing anything would spook Alayna's mother. Levi banished the mental pictures of her. That part still shook him.

"Another vessel came too close. Someone onboard was trouble. I don't know." His worried gaze narrowed. "If you're going to kill me, get it over with." He crossed himself as if preparing for the worst.

"How were you supposed to get back to the city?" Casey demanded. "Are the lifeboats intact?"

"The boat that brought you here. I can help you get back," he offered hopefully, looking from Levi to Casey, "if you let me go."

"We'll have more questions," Levi warned.

"I just want to go home."

Casey ushered Levi into the corridor. "We need this guy," she whispered. "He's the only connection we've got."

"Agreed." They couldn't let him out of their sight and they sure couldn't let the local authorities get their hands on him just yet.

After being untied, the sole survivor led the way topside. They walked through the scattered bodies. The scene rattled Levi though he'd walked through it once already.

"Here." Their guide gestured to a rope-style ladder mounted to the deck railing.

"Throw this overboard and climb down. The boat is waiting."

Casey checked over the railing to see if he was telling the truth. She gave Levi a confirming nod.

"You go first," he said to the man.

The only man to survive this massacre turned, but rather than walking to the railing, he dove for the nearest body, snatched the weapon lying next to it.

"Put it down!" Casey warned.

Both had a bead on the desperate man. Levi didn't want to shoot him. They needed him. "Just put down the weapon," he urged. "You'll get to go home. You have my word."

"I can't go back," the man said, his voice quavering. "I have failed." He stuck the silenced barrel to his temple. "I am dead already."

"No!" Casey shouted.

But she was too late. He'd pulled the trigger.

Damn. Oh, damn. Levi lowered his weapon.

Casey rubbed her eyes. "What the hell is going on here?"

Levi checked the poor bastard's pockets.

No ID, no cell. He stood and stared out across the water. "I don't know, but whatever it is, we have to stop it."

For that, they would need help.

Chapter Sixteen

Acapulco Airport, 2:00 p.m.

Casey entered the security checkpoint, Stark behind her, and thanked the heavens there was no long line. She just wanted this over with.

Had it only been hours ago that they'd left the yacht? Making shore had taken several minutes but it had seemed endless. They'd said nothing as the boat split through the blue water. Casey had decided both of them had been a little dazed. And a whole lot confused.

Once they'd stepped onto land, Casey had arranged for her rental car in Pozos to be picked up and she'd called the hotel there to take care of her room. Stark had done the same.

Since they were able to get flights

around three o'clock, there hadn't been a lot of time. A quick shower at the hotel in Acapulco and a change of clothes. They had checked out, grabbed some lunch and headed to the airport.

Every minute, every step had been together as a team. She'd managed to get a call in to Lucas while Stark was in the shower. Lucas had been in a meeting at the Colby Agency so she'd left a message that she would be in Chicago tonight and wanted to drop by the office to see him. It would be late, around eleven. She suggested they go to a late dinner and catch up on all her news. She'd chosen her words carefully so as not to arouse suspicions in case Victoria was in the room when he got the message but he would know the urgency by Casey's need to see him so late.

She hadn't heard back. Since her cell phone was long gone, there was no way for him to contact her now that she'd left the hotel room.

Casey suspected Stark had called his employer while she was in the shower as well. She'd thought she heard his voice at one point. She'd been tempted to eavesdrop but decided against it.

They had made it through this together. She'd figured she owed him her respect.

While checking out at the hotel's front desk, she had overheard some of the staff discussing the bodies found on the yacht just outside the bay. There were already rumors that drug transport was involved. Casey and Stark had separated themselves from that tragedy just in time.

Now it was time for the final separation.

"Well." Casey sighed. "I guess this is goodbye." They were traveling via different airlines to their destinations so the best thing was to get this part over with here at the security checkpoint. Why her heart felt as if it were swelling out of her chest she didn't know. This whole mission had been crazy like that.

Stark accepted her offered hand. "Guess so."

That wild, tingly sensation rushed up from her hand and spread through her entire body like a California brush fire out of control. The ability to breathe shut down. Casey felt as if she were drowning.

Her fingers clenched around his hand…
She didn't want to let go.

"We should make a pact," she said
abruptly, her knees shaking. This was
crazy! She was crazy. But she had to do
something. This couldn't be goodbye.

"What kind of pact?" He searched her
face with those remarkable green eyes.
She didn't miss the glimmer of anticipation there. He didn't really want this to be
goodbye either.

"In one month we'll meet somewhere."
They had kept their secrets. No addresses
or phone numbers exchanged and certainly
not employers' names. At this point, the addresses and phone numbers weren't really
relevant to protecting their clients but she
didn't want to be the one to ask. This was
as far out on the proverbial limb as she was
willing to go.

"Where?"

"How about New York." She laughed.
"At the top of the Empire State building.
Like in that old movie."

"We'll have dinner?" he suggested.

Who cared about eating as long as she
could listen to his voice and look into his

eyes? Reality intruded, stomping all over her enthusiasm. This was a mistake. She couldn't trust relationships and what he wanted her to believe was real. She'd end up getting kicked in the heart again. *Dumb, dumb idea, Casey.* No one was this nice for real.

"Dinner and maybe catch a play?" She managed a shaky breath. Didn't matter what she said now. It wasn't real. "This will all be behind us and we can reveal all our secrets then." She laughed again, way too nervous. Pathetic.

He smiled, stealing her breath all over again. "You're on. One month from today. Eight o'clock?"

She nodded. Casey would be herself again by then. It would be nice to see him, they would laugh and then say goodbye. Or maybe he wouldn't even show. No. She knew Levi Stark. He would show. If anyone bowed out it would have to be her. That would be the proper choice.

"Eight o'clock." She drew her hand from his. "See you then."

Before she could say or do anything else totally stupid, she turned and walked away.

Her eyes burned like crazy and she still couldn't breathe.

What was wrong with her?

Keep walking, she told herself. *Don't look back.*

"Casey!"

She stopped. She closed her eyes a second, then worked up the nerve to face him. He waited right behind her.

"I can't let you go without..." He stared at her a moment as if lost for words.

Then he kissed her.

She should have run away. This was another mega mistake. But she couldn't do it. She dropped her bag and put her arms around his neck. He tasted like sweetened coffee and the chocolate he'd had for dessert after lunch. But mostly he tasted like Stark. And she wanted to taste all of him. His arms felt so good around her...she could stay this way for...ever.

He drew back, pressed his forehead to hers.

What was she doing? Nothing was forever.

Say goodbye, Casey!

"FYI," he murmured, "that was real. See you in one month."

Casey watched him walk away.

Something deep inside her shifted.

She was going to miss him.

She'd been outdone, there was no denying it. That truth had her surrendering to a smile. She had a feeling he was right.

Levi Stark was the real thing.

Chapter Seventeen

The Colby Agency, 5:51 p.m.

Lucas had gotten Casey's message.

He collapsed into the chair behind his desk. Thank God. He and Thomas had been ready to send a team to find her. Lucas had been worried sick.

Since the Colby Agency staff meeting ended, he'd tried returning Casey's call several times. Her cell had gone straight to voice mail. He doubted he would be able to reach her before her arrival in Chicago.

Victoria wouldn't question his need to meet an old colleague for a drink. No matter how hard he tried, Lucas couldn't get past this massive lump of guilt hanging somewhere between his throat and his heart.

Casey had news. Good or bad, he would

need to share it with Victoria. He shouldn't have kept her in the dark like this.

He stood. There was no time like the present to right this wrong. As if his troubled thoughts had summoned her, his door opened and Victoria walked in. Generally her arrival wouldn't startle him. Tonight it did. The guilt was weighing heavy.

"Victoria." He smiled, though the weight in his chest made that simple gesture difficult.

"Lucas, I…" She held up her hands as if defeated.

She looked as worried as he felt. "Has something happened?"

His wife settled into the chair in front of his desk. "Yes," she said finally. "And we have to talk about it."

Lucas lowered into his chair. Worry fisted in his chest. What had his preoccupation with Keaton caused him to miss? "We'll talk about anything you want for as long as you want."

Her worried gaze settled on his. "I made a mistake."

Lucas wanted to rush around his desk and hold her. To reassure his beloved wife that he would protect her and love her no matter what mistake she felt she had committed. He had made a rather large one himself.

This was nonsense. He moved around his desk to join Victoria. He took her hand in his. "Tell me what's wrong." He couldn't bear to see her so worried.

"Like you, I've continued to have my reservations about Keaton."

Anger unfurled in Lucas's gut. This had gone on far too long.

"So I sent Stark to look into a man named Paulo Fernandez in Pozos."

For the first time in his life, Lucas was speechless.

"I know," she urged, taking his surprise for something it wasn't, "that I was the one to insist we stop looking for trouble where he's concerned. But I had to do this. I knew how concerned you've been about him."

"Have you heard from Stark?"

She nodded. "Finally. I hadn't heard from him since his arrival in Mexico. I was beginning to grow anxious. But he's on his way back. He left a message that he would be giving me a full briefing tonight and I'd like you to be a part of it. Whatever he has learned, we should face it together."

Lucas squeezed her hand. "I love you for caring so much, my darling."

She shook her head. "I should have told you. It was foolhardy of me to go this route." She peered into his eyes, hers hopeful. "Can you forgive me?"

Dear, dear Victoria. How did he tell her that he had done precisely the same thing?

"There is something I need to tell you as well." She looked at him expectantly. "I believe we can most likely call it even."

They shared a good laugh over their foolish decisions and then they hugged. Deep inside, they both understood that tonight's news would not be good.

Chapter Eighteen

11:05 p.m.

Levi emerged from the taxi and walked straight through the front entrance. He waved to security as he headed for the bank of elevators to go to the fourth floor.

He was exhausted, physically and mentally.

He'd tried to sleep on the plane but the bizarre events in Mexico wouldn't let that happen.

And he couldn't get Casey out of his head.

She was…he stalled…standing at the elevators. Of his building.

What was she doing here?

The chime announcing an elevator had arrived sounded, snapping him out of the daze he'd lapsed into. The doors opened and Casey stepped through, apparently in a daze of her own. Levi hurried to catch up, barely getting through the doors before they closed.

Casey looked up, startled. "Stark. What're you doing here?"

Levi had the presence of mind to press the button for the fourth floor. The elevator doors closed and the car glided upward. He met her gaze. "This is where I work."

"The Colby Agency? Oh, my God. Who sent you on this mission?"

He hesitated a moment. The mission was over now. They were both here at the Colby Agency—somehow. What difference did it make? "Victoria Colby-Camp, the head of the agency."

Astonishment claimed Casey's face. "Victoria sent you?"

That same astonishment surely claimed his. "You know Victoria?"

"Her husband is my godfather."

"Lucas?" This moment was like the rest of their mission…crazy.

She nodded. "He didn't want Victoria to know. That's why I'm meeting him here at this hour."

The elevator stopped on the fourth floor and the doors opened. "I guess we're about to blow both their covers because I'm meeting Victoria."

The next few minutes were a little unnerving and a whole lot strange. Like everything about his and Casey's time together so far. Victoria and Lucas had asked her son, Jim, to sit in on the briefing.

"That's all Alayna relayed to you?" Lucas asked. "You're absolutely certain there was nothing more?"

"Positive," Levi assured him. He'd given a word-for-word account of the meeting with Alayna and his questioning by the woman referred to as the Dragon. Casey had done the same. Then, they had both shared their shock at just how much the woman resembled Victoria.

Victoria had taken it all in good stride. She seemed to maintain a proper perspective but the whole business had to be terrifying on some level.

"What do you make of this, Lucas?" Jim asked.

"The Dragon has been a part of the international intelligence world for a very long time. Longer than me." He looked from one to the other, his gaze coming to rest on Victoria. Levi noticed his eyes softened. "We had a brief affair some thirty years ago when I was a green field operative. I never encountered her again after that. The rumor was that she had turned. Gone to the dark side, so to speak. I can't even recall the last time I saw her. Until we were in Mexico last month. I was certain I saw her in the crowd. She was there one moment and then she was gone." He shrugged. "I decided I was mistaken. Apparently I was right the first time."

"There have been rumors about the Dragon," Casey spoke up, "but I wasn't so sure she was real until last night. She's real." Casey turned to Lucas then. "She hates you, Lucas. I could see it in her eyes, hear it in her voice, when she questioned me."

"You were unable to confirm that she is Keaton's mother?" Victoria asked, sounding strong in spite of present circumstances.

"That's correct," Levi told her. "But that was the thinking of Fernandez, the contact in Pozos. He had a direct connection to the

Dragon which leads me to believe he knew what he was talking about and that she was indeed Keaton's mother."

"It makes sense," Victoria said, seeming distracted now. "Keaton insinuated himself into our lives. He has been watching you," she said to Lucas, "all this time. His alleged mother, a woman with whom you had an affair thirty years ago, despises you. Could she have sent him to finally have some sort of revenge?"

Jim shook his head before Lucas could answer. "But why wait so long? He's had ample opportunity to complete his mission, if he'd had a specific one."

Levi had heard the story of how Jim Colby had returned over seven years ago to exact his misguided revenge. He would know that strategy better than anyone. His point was valid.

Victoria was the one shaking her head now. The confusion and uncertainty on her face were way out of character. "Lucas recently retired," she offered. "Perhaps she stationed Keaton here to watch until just the right moment. Perhaps she doesn't want Lucas to be happily retired…with a wife and family." Victoria rested her gaze on her husband, the confusion and uncertainty shifting to a palpable worry. "Since your encounter was brief, does she have another reason to hate you that much? Did you, in the line of duty, take someone she loved?"

"Not to my knowledge." Lucas looked equally stricken by the turn the events surrounding Keaton and this mission had taken. "She was a source who provided much needed intelligence in missions that might otherwise have failed, but that was a very long time ago. She vanished. The rumors since have connected her to ruthless criminal activity. None, to my knowledge, has ever been corroborated. Until last month I had no reason to believe that she was even still alive."

"There's an avenue we're missing," Jim suggested. All attention settled on him. "This entire setup could be related to your connections in Washington, Lucas. That may be what this waiting game has been about. Settling in and then striking at just the right moment."

Silence reigned for several seconds.

"That's possible," Lucas admitted. "I

suppose all the coincidences, like Victoria's abduction and what happened in Pozos last month, could be building toward a goal." He shook his head. "But it doesn't feel right. It feels personal."

"Whatever it is," Victoria announced, sounding more like the strong woman Levi had come to know, "we have to stop Keaton and this woman who calls herself the Dragon."

"We need to learn their ultimate intent ASAP," Jim suggested. "That knowledge is crucial to moving forward. I'm convinced that's why we haven't gotten even close to what we need on Keaton in all this time."

"Agreed." Lucas gave a resolute nod. "We need your uncle," he said to Casey, "and his team of specialists to find the Dragon and bring her to justice. It's past time if even half the rumors are true."

"My uncle," Casey offered, "may require my and Stark's assistance, since we're the only ones who've seen her recently."

Levi was surprised by her suggestion though he was thinking the same. "I would like to see this through," he said to Victoria.

"This task will require all our resources,

I fear." Victoria reached for her husband's hand. "And much strength."

"Casey, Stark," Jim said, "you two did a brilliant job with limited resources." He looked to each person gathered around his mother's conference table. "But now we have a far bigger mission ahead of us.

"Lucas will coordinate our efforts with those of the CIA. Stark, you and Casey will provide whatever support is needed on the ground. First thing in the morning I'll put Ian Michaels and Simon Ruhl, our agency's seconds in command," he said for Casey's benefit, "on following up in Mexico. With their contacts we may be able to learn some additional information." Jim looked from Victoria to Lucas and back. "I want the two of you to have round-the-clock security. We don't know what this woman might have planned."

"And Keaton," Victoria added, "with what we've learned, he may be an equally dangerous threat."

"I'm about to pay him a visit—if he hasn't vanished as well." Jim stood. "The sooner I have his activities under surveillance, the better I'll feel. For all we know, he could be in danger as well." He surveyed those around the table once more. "We will neutralize this threat."

Victoria and Lucas exchanged a look. "Together," she stated with all the strength and courage for which she was known.

He squeezed her hand. "Always."

WHEN THE BRIEFING HAD concluded, Levi shared the elevator back to the lobby with Casey.

"Do you have to return to Langley immediately?" He hoped not. She'd said she was on vacation.

"Depends on how quickly we get this new mission off the ground."

If Levi was really lucky he'd be right beside her for that one. "Looks like we might be partners again."

"I don't have a problem with that."

Her comment had hope expanding in his chest. "You planning to stay at a hotel while you're here?" he ventured. Or maybe she planned to stay with Victoria and Lucas.

"Don't have any plans."

"It's late." Well after midnight. He didn't

like the idea of her looking for a hotel at this hour. "I know you're exhausted."

She eyed him curiously. "Is there an invitation in there somewhere?"

"Yes. You're welcome to stay at my place for as long as you're here." He decided to take it all the way. "Whenever you're here."

"I warn you," she teased, "I can be a serious pain in the butt a lot of the time."

"I know." He snagged her hand and drew her close. "And you always have to have the last word."

"Yeah." She pressed her palms against his chest and slid her hands up and around his neck. "There's just one problem."

He searched her eyes, smiled at how they glittered with expectation. "What's that?"

"There's a sizeable hole in your strategy." She leaned into him. His body reacted hard and fast. "You see, I realized something about myself recently. I have trust issues. I have to be certain this is real. That could be a big problem."

"You're right. That is a problem." He pulled her closer, his heart pounding so hard he couldn't breathe. "And I gladly accept the challenge of correcting that situation." He lowered his lips to hers and kissed her with all the feelings churning wildly inside him.

He had every intention of teaching Casey just how real this could be.

Starting right now.

Chapter Nineteen

When Jim and the others had at last left Victoria's office, she moved to her treasured window and stared out at the familiar scene, emotions churning inside her. Lucas stood silently behind her. He was no doubt reeling with similar emotions. This woman—this Dragon—who looked so much like Victoria wanted to destroy Lucas. Whatever her motives, she appeared to have vast resources.

That was the part that terrified Victoria the most.

She had to be stopped.

Was Slade Keaton innocent on some level in all this? Victoria couldn't stop thinking of how Jim had been brainwashed into wanting to kill Victoria for wrongs she had not committed. Was this woman using her own son the same way? Was that why Keaton watched Lucas so closely? Victoria had observed his fascination with Lucas on more than one occasion. Dear God, what did all this mean? What kind of mother would do this to her son?

Lucas's hands settled on Victoria's shoulders and turned her to face him. "I want you safe." The worry in his voice and eyes tore at her heart. "My history with the CIA is the issue here. I won't have that past putting you in danger."

Was he suggesting she hide while he stood and fought this evil? Victoria forced the quaking inside her to calm. Those runaway emotions would work against her reasoning. She needed her head clear. "Are you sure this is about your past with the Agency? Or is it about your decision to choose me as your wife?"

A frown furrowed across his weary brow. "That moment she and I shared was a very long time ago, Victoria. I've been over it and over it and I can't pinpoint a single reason she would show up now seeking revenge." He sighed. "Unless, as you suggested, someone I didn't know was connected to her was a victim in some capacity or another with one of my covert missions."

Victoria took his face in her hands. She loved this man so very much. He wanted to protect her. "We can't ignore the fact that she and I share numerous physical features, Lucas. That carries some significance that we can't just set aside."

An old ache surfaced in his eyes. "When I first met her, in the line of duty, I was stunned at how much the two of you looked alike." He shrugged. "In truth, that's likely why that moment happened in the first place."

Victoria smiled sadly. She knew Lucas had been in love with her for a very long time. But she had been married to James then. She'd pretended not to notice the way Lucas looked at her. He'd always been the perfect gentleman, even well after James's death.

"In that case, perhaps it's me she wants out of the way. Maybe Keaton's fascination with you has been a ruse. If I were out of the picture, she might have a chance to rekindle that old flame." Before Lucas could argue, Victoria added, "People with obsessions sometimes cross that murky line called reality. We can't be sure. Maybe she didn't send Keaton at all." The way the woman had questioned Casey and Levi certainly made it sound that way. "He may have grown up in your shadow—in the shadow of his mother's obsession. Perhaps he believes somehow that getting me out of the way and delivering you to her would elevate his standing in her eyes."

Lucas pulled her into his arms. Her heart reacted. "The fact is," he said softly, that same fear and worry she'd been feeling clear in his eyes, "we don't know what he wants and how he's connected to her or even what she wants. We have a little scrambled information and a whole lot of hard questions. What counts is that we stay safe while finding the truth."

Victoria managed a smile. "You're right. That's what counts."

Lucas hugged her close. Victoria closed her eyes and inhaled his familiar, masculine scent.

They had waited a very long time and

suffered a great deal before finding the happiness they now shared.

No one was going to take that away from them.

The ruse had diverted and hindered their efforts for a time, but the Colby Agency was on the case now.

* * * * *

LARGER-PRINT BOOKS!
GET 2 FREE LARGER-PRINT NOVELS PLUS
2 FREE GIFTS!

◆ Harlequin®

INTRIGUE®
BREATHTAKING ROMANTIC SUSPENSE

HILPI1B